"This may one be the first novels to talk about this issue from the women's point of view, and in a very effective way...*Blood of the Dawn* is an original addition to the abundant literature on this difficult and polemic episode of our recent history." —JAVIER AGREDA, *LA REPUBLIC*

"I have to control the pain at my center, absorb it until it disappears and dissipates in a vapor without weight or consequence. Dominate my flesh, my eyes, their skin. The body itself does not exist. What exists is a forceful act. A retaliation from the State. A gestating woman. Pieces of an informer. Bits of a traitor. There are also (they always say) massacres. Devastation. Quotas. Papers, letters, one atop the other, mounting with excessive order. Discipline exists. The word exists but doesn't hurt. It cuts, but doesn't hurt. Kills, but doesn't hurt. Genocidal explosion. Hammer and sickle. The red sun. The dawn."

"An original novel...Lyrical and cinematographic. If there are certain things that can't be (shouldn't be) told with words, we cannot silence them either." —SOPHIE CANAL

BLOOD OF THE DAWN

BLOOD
OF THE DAWN

—

Claudia Salazar Jiménez

TRANSLATED FROM THE SPANISH BY
ELIZABETH BRYER

DEEP VELLUM PUBLISHING

DALLAS, TEXAS

Deep Vellum Publishing
3000 Commerce St., Dallas, Texas 75226
deepvellum.org · @deepvellum

Deep Vellum Publishing is a 501C3
nonprofit literary arts organization founded in 2013.

ISBN: 978-1-941920-42-8 (paperback) · 978-1-941920-43-5 (ebook)
LIBRARY OF CONGRESS CONTROL NUMBER: 2016948061

—

Cover design & typesetting by Anna Zylicz · annazylicz.com

Text set in Bembo, a typeface modeled on typefaces cut by Francesco Griffo
for Aldo Manuzio's printing of *De Aetna* in 1495 in Venice.

Distributed by Consortium Book Sales & Distribution.

Printed in the United States of America on acid-free paper.

For Ana Ribeiro

Never, human men,
was there so much pain in the chest, in the lapel, in the wallet,
in the glass, in the butcher's shop, in arithmetic!
Never so much painful affection,
never did the distance charge so close

CÉSAR VALLEJO

○●

"Everyone who knows anything of history also knows that great social revolutions are impossible without the feminine ferment."

MARX

○●

blackout total darkness Where was it? all over Where did it come from? high tension towers fell to their knees bombs explode all raze blast burst Were you with the group? cooking at home while I waited for my husband blackout typing up the meeting's minutes blackout developing some photos blackout get candles I don't have enough six pages two towers the outskirts of the capital What did you say? you can't sign comrade darkness excluded from history submit or blow up bomb Did you find out what they did? wow you cleaned your whole plate smile no candles eat three towers they say now more time more towers When will there be light again? candles turn on the radio I can't find the matches three candles no matches make a spark with flint just kidding bomb we have a generator go to the epicenter where what we can't see is happening bomb report what's happening on the other side of the towers see Where were each of the three of them? blackout

○●

They brought me to this jail in the capital not long before our leadership fell. They almost always bring me to this room so Major Romero can interrogate me. Everything is white, whiter than a hospital. The three chairs. The table with the white melamine top. White walls, too. It's already almost two weeks since I found out they'd caught them. I wonder what they've done to Comrade Leader. Fucking dogs. If they touch him, they're all going to die; one by one we'll take them down.

The only sound is the clock. Romero hasn't shown up yet. It's a bit chilly in this white room. Such a difference from that sandy place where I started my social work. I especially remember one day when the sun tested us. Unbearable, hellish. That's what the heat felt like on that long stretch of sand settled by so many people. I was there with the engineer who coordinated the construction projects and with Fernanda, the social worker. I'd also taken along my four-year-old daughter. I thought it would be good for her to play with children who had little or nothing.

The sandy ground stretched on and on, a boiling yellow cloak. The heat was stifling. I felt the sweat of my girl's tiny hand in mine. One of the people in charge of the housing committee handed me a glass of water to relieve her thirst. Water was sold at the price of gold, off-loaded from trucks that came barely once a week. The glass that my daughter had just finished meant less water for one of these children.

She was more settled now so I left her with the other little ones and joined the community members to discuss the upcoming projects. They needed a network of potable water, drainage and public lighting to cover at least ten streets. They had also asked the municipality for a health post with basic services and for a school to be built. Education is fundamental to breaking free from the structural inequalities that social organization is founded on; without it, the potential for change *Mami!!!* is practically non-existent. My years of experience as an educator give me the authority to confirm *Mamiiiiiiiiii!!!!* that without the appropriate level of *Señora Marcela, your daughter!*

I ran to where the children were playing. My daughter was stock-still in the middle of the sandy area, her little legs trembling in fright, almost not breathing, hiccupping, her face soaked in tears. She had fallen over in a spot where sand had mixed with compacted earth and it was hard to stay upright. When she saw me, she stretched out her little arms and let fly a loud, distressed wail: *Mami, there's no ground here, carry me!*

I picked her up and pressed her to my chest. She held on to me tight. Her little heart beat fast as a frightened bird's. I wiped the sweat and tears from her face. I stroked her head and picked out the grains of sand that had nestled among strands of her hair. *Calm down, I'm here now, nothing bad is going to happen,* I said. I stroked her temples in a way that always relaxed her and she calmed down bit by bit. The children clustered around us on that lost stretch of desert: no shoes, threadbare clothes, barefooted on the hot sand, hardly any water and not a single complaint. For them there really was no ground beneath their feet. We couldn't waste time on trivialities when there was so much to do. *Alright, now, stop crying, we're brave girls.*

"Teacher, how are you today?" Major Romero says, coming in out of the blue. He always calls me this. I humor him to see if he'll let slip more about our Leader; I have a sneaking suspicion our future's in his hands.

"Good morning, Major. Here I am, all ready for us to talk."

Romero settles into the chair opposite me. He smiles. I have only two weapons left: my patience and my silence.

"Teacher, I've had the pleasure of getting to know you over the past few days, and I've come to see that you're very persistent. You're tenacious and strong-willed, a rock." Romero shifts his weight in the chair as if wanting to say something confidential. He leans toward me a little and says, his voice almost a whisper, "That's why you had access to the Standing Committee, right?"

○●

Their most important work was making decisions in the midst of war. Our one and only ideological line decided it. Comrade Leader, Comrade Number Two, and Comrade Number Three: a perfect trinity. Comrade Leader is the One, the Guiding Thought of our revolution. Comrade Two was the person who brought me into the party. Comrade Three was in charge of logistics. Three. A perfect, sacred number. A closed Circle. The Standing Committee. Organized secrecy at the epicenter.

The revolution couldn't wait any longer; sitting and waiting on reactions is what the State wants. To substitute one class for another, one number for another. Thought rules, but Mao said it: "Power grows out of the barrel of a gun." Our military arm, Comrade Felipe, was a restless colt itching for combat. He said that in some rural communities, people had reacted negatively to the revolutionary doctrine.

Some found it difficult to accept the revolution, but we trusted they would absorb and grow to understand the Guiding Thought. There were clashes and some comrades fell, which emboldened police in zones key to our advancement. At that meeting, I remember how Comrade Felipe showed Comrade Three one of the FAL infantry rifles we had seized.

"This is what power is made of, comrade, feel it."

It had been a long time since she'd held one. Now she focused on politics and theory, on what endures when arms are laid down. It didn't feel so heavy to her, but its bulk braced her arm. Quick as anything, she unloaded and reloaded it. Then, as if suddenly uncomfortable, she gave it back to Comrade Felipe. The Leader prepared to speak to the assembled commissars and open the meeting. *Comrades, it must be made clear from the first: the party rules over the barrel of the gun and we will never let it be the other way around. That said, the masses need to be educated on the crucible of Marxist-Leninist-Maoist thought, and the revolutionary army must mobilize the masses. Forceful measures are needed to take the qualitative leap of decisive importance for the party and for the revolution. To transform the orderless agrarian masses into an organized militia.* Comrade Leader paused to observe people's reactions. Not one murmur. Respectful silence in response to his words. Comrade Two maintained an unreadable look. Her posture was always erect, vertical, in line with the wall, where there was an image of Mao guiding his people beneath the red sun in perpetual advancement and transformation. A new dawn unfolding. Comrade Leader continued outlining the ideological plan. Comrade Felipe would be in charge of the tactical details this time, of overseeing how the action should proceed.

The place had already been decided. The colt felt liberated and clenched the FAL rifle harder, the veins in his hands bulging.

Objective: to deprive our enemies of their undeserved upper hand, forcing them into submission. May our actions speak for themselves. They're either with us or against us. Annihilate. We will start tearing down the walls and unleashing the Dawn. It will send a strong message. They're not expecting this. Comrade Leader announced the name of the hamlet: *Lucanamarca.*

"Lucanamarca," echoed Number Three, her voice raised almost to a shout, her fist in the air. Comrade Two looked at me with disquiet. She had let a few seconds go by without reacting and now lifted her fist in the air as well, reiterating the one and only decision.

"Lucanamarca."

○●

how many were there it hardly matters twenty came thirty say those who got away counting is useless crack machete blade a divided chest crack no more milk another one falls machete knife dagger stone sling crack my daughter crack my brother crack my husband crack my mother crack exposed flesh broken neck machete eyeball crack femur tibia fibula crack faceless earless noseless swallow it crack right now eat it up pick the ear up off the floor don't spit it out don't crack five put them in a line machete crack blood soup spattering making mud their boots slipping comrade crack screaming screeching machete bones crack just ten were enough rope arms up you reek fetid crack you reek they reek your feet their cunts sebum machete blow mud the floor chop chop penises testicles for your old mother to eat up open your mouth crack for pity's sake machete blow there's no money for bullets crack campesinos machete blow the party is god crack lip tooth throat blade blade blade ax blow crack ten enough machete blow crack the earth is soaked she can't take any more blood crack pachamama vomits liquid of the people crack one's escaping with a baby crack four months crack machete blow mother's back howling shut up stab eye it won't come out at last you've shut up bitch crack baby on the floor crack heavy stone soft skull baby crack three months crack lucanamarca

○●

You head to the *yunza* happy as can be with Justina and Dominga. Thrilled, the three of you, to be off to the celebration to see what your presents will be this time. Justina wants to make the most of the occasion to meet up with Vicente from the other hamlet. She has a thing for him. Last time she managed to talk to him for a bit. Dominga has stepped out in her best dress for Fabián, it's looking like they'll move in together soon. Dominga told you that Fabián wrote love poems for her, that he called her his little vicuña and was really affectionate. Dominga's fortunate to have landed such a catch—the councilor's son, mind you. She's so lucky, your dear friend. They've invited you to come along to see if you might meet someone for yourself.

Chicha flows like the hamlet's river, plentiful, spilling laughter and jubilance throughout the community. You've put on the little red hat that your father Samuel just gave you for your sixteenth birthday. Mariano says you look pretty in red.

You're gorgeous, sweet cousin, give me a little kiss. He winds streamers around you; you let them fall free. How much chicha has Mariano had to drink? He wants a little kiss, he says. He's crazy. The chicha makes him crazy. Your cousin is strong and also a good woodcutter: with one swing of the ax he parts the logs. He will probably be the one to fell the tree; he'll fell it whole. He has thick eyebrows and eyes that look around and all over like a condor. He's agile and strong as a puma.

You taste a little sip of chicha and at once your cheeks flush red; you've gone all rosy-faced, Modesta. *Sweet rosy cheeks*, says a young man you've just met. You laugh but you don't say anything, you just lower your eyes and then keep them on Mariano, who has started dancing with the Huarotos' daughter. This young man says his name is Gaitán and he doesn't leave your side for the rest of the celebration. Everyone dances around the tree, which is chock-full of colorful balloons, fluttering streamers, and presents. Which one will be yours? Everyone forms a circle and dances to the right. They halt. To the left; dancing, dancing. They move toward the tree and now move away. Forward and back. Hand in hand, the community dances. Gaitán breaks from the circle to swing the ax but, oh no, it doesn't even make a mark on the tree. *You have to put your back into it, you fledgling!* the Quechán brothers yell out, making faces. When it's Mariano's turn, the tree booms and a present even falls from the trunk. *Bring it down, champ, bring it down!* He swings twice more and the tree topples. The community all over its branches among the streamers, the presents, and the popping balloons.

○●

Ana María Balducci's parties have always stirred up a weird mix of love and hate in me. Getting an invite is a routine event. The faces and bodies are the usual suspects: minimal variation. A new face might join the gathering after passing through whichever filters occur to Ana María, but she would rather avoid change. It's a pagan temple where we can cavort without pause. There aren't many of us, never more than fourteen. A party among friends: it sounds good, saying it like that. No complications for anyone. *Melanie, darling, congratulations on your fabulous article last week.* The aspiring congresswoman always praises my work. She's the only politician who comes to our parties, and she counts on our discretion to pave her way to Congress. I do my work, investigate, capture images, try to shine a light on what's been overlooked. Not long ago I collaborated on a story about a certain corruption case in a government department. Now there's nothing for it but to wait on the judiciary to do its job, though I don't expect too much from them. Almost nothing, to tell the truth. I'm getting another vodka. I like being here.

I watch them all dancing, chatting, drinking. The party is a bubble. If it were up to these women, many of them would spend their lives in Europe or Miami. They stay here in this city of drizzle because they know all too well that the bubble wouldn't be so small, or so exclusive, elsewhere. Maybe the bubble is a prison, too. *Camila, have you heard that my nephew Ricardo is applying to the Navy Officers School? He wants to be an admiral, just like your papá.* Yes, darling, yes. And Camila has taken mental note no doubt, don't you worry about that. No need to ask explicitly.

Tomorrow bright and early she'll talk to her father and just happen to mention your nephew. He'll make a fine officer for sure. How positively wonderful it is to be here.

I slide onto another sofa. They're talking about the latest news. *It was a massacre. They didn't even spare the children.* Their faces show astonishment overlaid with horror. *What on earth are those guerrillas after?* Someone drags hard on a cigarette. Another puffs furiously. Together they say, *Guerrillas? What harm can a baby do?* The rest listen with feigned attention. The aspiring congresswoman wants more information. *Ana María, surely you're better informed, tell us about what's happening in the mountains.*

Silence ensues as all eyes turn toward the hostess. The Balducci family owns the most powerful TV network in the country. Frowning in irritation, Ana María crosses her arms and says, "Why, communists are what's happening, ladies. Really red, really radical. They're recruiting campesinos and planning a so-called people's war in the mountains. Nothing to worry about; I expect that in a few weeks the Army will have taken care of everything."

"If they recruit campesinos, then why did they just massacre them?" someone asks.

"Perhaps some tussle over land. Sometimes mountain people fight over any little thing and they can be violent when resolving their disputes. If you want to know more," she says with a smile that concludes the topic, "watch the news bulletin."

Someone has started to dance to the beat of David Bowie to placate Ana María; it's not in anyone's interest to fall out with her. The atmosphere is a little tense. Not even Bowie manages to relax it. No more politics or favors for tonight. Let's dance a little.

Talk, drink. I'd rather be at Kraken. It's still early. I stir my vodka lime with the cherry. The liquid swirls. Why massacre those you're supposedly trying to recruit? Something doesn't fit. Why did Ana María get so annoyed? Linking campesinos and violence has been a broken record since colonial times. What must be happening up there, really? Without warning Ana María moves toward me. Her perfume is unmistakable.

"You're mighty pensive tonight, is something up?"

"Do you really believe that all the trouble in the mountains is a matter of violent campesinos?"

"Come on, enough about that already. Look, I'll tell you something I know will make you ridiculously happy. You know who's here in the city?"

"A lot of people, I'd think. You and I, for example."

"Oh Mel, don't be such a pain. You'll see, I'll tell you and you'll drop the comedy act."

"I'm listening."

"I'm not telling you now," she plays the part of a sulky child, but one of my best smiles wins her over.

"Alright then, if you smile at me like that, I'll tell you: Daniela's here."

"..."

"She wants to see you."

○●

Five in the afternoon in the city of drizzle. The warmth of the café protects us from the humidity, from the fishbowl we live in. The voices, the wine glasses, and the silverware come together in a kind of café-wide choreography. Why did I agree to see her? Why right now? Daniela gets here at last. Radiant, as if the sun dwelled in her movements and shone through her skin. For a few seconds, the murmur of conversation drops off and in that sudden silence all eyes converge on our table. I tell her she looks beautiful. Straight up, no metaphors. She smiles. The murmuring starts up again and builds, as if everyone has shaken themselves awake. The voices, the wine glasses, the cups, and the spoons reprise their dance. *Let's see if now you'll tell me why you stopped talking to me.* Why did I stop talking to you? *You disappeared, as if the earth had swallowed you whole.* Honestly, Dani, I'm not sure. I don't remember. It was so long ago. Some things make less sense with time. It's not worth raking over. Instead, tell me about your latest exhibition. Daniela Miller, the first female Peruvian painter to have her own show in Paris. *It was incredible, tons of people came.* A huge success, from what I saw in the papers. Ana María sent her finest correspondent to cover the opening and they broadcast it on El Noticiero. *Everybody was there. The only person missing was President Mitterrand.* She says it as a joke but I think deep down she wanted him there. She smiles. She keeps telling me about it, that no doubt other Peruvian painters are being eaten up with envy, that now the French will value Peruvian art for sure, that next up is London, Paris, New York, she's ready to take on the world. Plans, projects, life.

Why did I stop talking to you? I remember your breath sharing the rhythm of my kisses, my breath guided by the graze of your lips. Surrendering to the desire in your eyes. Delicate and soft creases. My fingers, lost, shipwrecked in your warm hollow. Turbulent waist, towed by the tide of my hands. The tense strings of our bodies dissolving in harp chords. Undulating serpents that thawed their defenses to coil together. Your marble neck chiseled by kisses, a sculpture of love. Eyes that lapped the river, the sea, waterfalls. Wine overflowing the glasses. Thirst. Punch-drunk lover. Skin glossy with dew. Your voice, body, name. Daniela. Daniela Miller.

The sun has come out, despite the drizzle. *I'm heading back tomorrow. If you come to Paris, let me know, got it? I don't want you disappearing on me again.*

○●

"Teacher, tell me about your relationship with Fernanda Rivas, who at one stage was Comrade Two. Living together so long, I imagine you became very close—intimate friends, even." Major Romero lights a cigarette. I make sure not to let on how the smoke irritates me. I can't show even the slightest hint of weakness.

"In the revolution we have comrades, not friends," I cut him off short.

"A matter of putting different names to things," Romero counters with a small smile that can't conceal his satisfaction at having annoyed me. He lets out a lungful of smoke that blears the room.

You're not going to find out a thing. If you know as much as you say you do, Major, then why ask? You don't need to know that Fernanda and I met a few months before the debacle in that sand-swept place. We had gotten bad news. We didn't get the funding for the community projects after all. The engineer shook his head slowly, eyes on the floor and not saying a word, thoroughly down-cast; the blueprints he'd drawn up without charging a cent lay on the table, ruffled by a dry breeze that blew into the room. One of the blueprints rolled up and fell to the floor. No one picked it up.

I bit my fist out of sheer rage. I was sick to death of false promises. *Marcela, it's just one project, if no one funds it now we'll find other ways to do it,* Fernanda said, mystifyingly serene. I could only work my jaw in fury. So much red tape, so many plans and promises. The sandy patch would go on being a no-man's-land. *Words count for nothing,* I said to Fernanda, my voice almost breaking. Another frustrated project with no funding or government support. One more, one of so many. I had lost count. Who cared, anyway? Who cared about us? *You're mistaken. Words have more power than you can imagine.* How could Fernanda believe in the power of words? How was that possible?

You'll also never know, little Romero, that I saw Fernanda almost every day. We worked together in the poorest parts on the outskirts of the capital, organizing projects for communities. At the Teachers' Union rallies we were always together. So many times the police's water-cannon trucks flung us to the ground with their blasts of water, but we kept pushing forward and resisting. And you'll never know, Major, that while Fernanda was very hard on herself and said little, her generosity was boundless. She was a workhorse, tireless when it came to organizing. Politics and revolution: that was all she talked about. Focused. Her mind centered on it. The perfect militant, ready to give her all for others. I watched her rise to the highest ranks of the armed struggle, to the peak of the Guiding Thought. The revolution made flesh.

I know what I'm talking about. Hold fast to your rage and hate. Keep them burning within. Hate will pave the way to great things.

Come with me to the Federation's auditorium next Friday and you'll find out what I'm talking about, Marcela. You'll see what words can do. That's where it all started. *Words are just hot air, but since you ask, I'll come.* You know nothing, Romero, and will never understand the heroism of Comrade Two.

○●

The auditorium was teeming with workers, teachers, and students. Seated at the center of the table was a man with thick tortoiseshell glasses that offset a calm, neutral expression. He had a teacherly air about him that made me imagine it would be a long afternoon. So much to do and here I was at a talk. I got comfortable beside Fernanda. Her expression had changed, had transformed, perhaps. I'd never seen her look that way at anyone. What was it? Her body stayed straight in her seat while her expectant pupils filled with light. What was happening to her?

When the professor with the thick glasses stood, his fluent delivery made me forget everything else. The things he said and the vigorous way he said them didn't fit with his academic bearing, and the brilliant way he weaved together ideas and connected them to reality was unsurpassable. A man who knew what he was talking about. The tapestry kept growing in a dance of ideas: class struggle, revolution, starting in the countryside, Mao, Lenin, Marx, Communist Party, no stopping until power is gained. His voice echoed in my head. *The fundamental objective is power. Lenin said it, comrades: "Everything is illusory except power."* Power. No stopping until it's ours. Believing in projects financed by others, in unions, in rallies, was illusory.

Nothing but illusory. Power was what was real. Was that what shone in Fernanda's eyes?

Applause announced the end and I dared to ask a question.

"Leaders of the group Red Nation say that we women will be in charge of feeding the troops." A few laughs ricocheted around the hall. "What I want to know, professor, is this: What role in the revolution does your party offer us women?"

He raised an eyebrow and adjusted his glasses, fixed his gaze on me and cleared his throat. *The incorporation of women into the production process, coupled with the deepening of the class struggle in this country, necessarily poses the central problem of the politicization of women as an integral part of the people's war. The State, increasingly reactionary, denies women the future. The only possible path for professional women is taking up the role that history demands of them as intellectuals: participating in the revolution.* I saw it all, as if a beaming light coming out of his throat had pierced the center of my chest and radiated within me to dispel any speck of darkness. His was the only path possible. His words could change the world, could write history. Women fully included in the revolution. Now I understood the sparkle in Fernanda's eyes.

"I have to meet him."

"No problem, Marcela. What about the three of us have dinner together?" Fernanda continued in a conspiratorial tone, "We've got plans we want to share with you."

"You know him?"

"I never said because it wouldn't have been wise then. He's my husband."

○●

Another *yunza* and then a few more. Gaitán came closer. You ran, Modesta, making your escape among the balloons, the dancers, the chicha drinkers, and the streamers. Another *yunza* and your cousin left your thoughts. Gaitán practiced swinging the ax. Some trees fell, others stood strong. Gaitán came with streamers in hand and wound them around you. You adjusted them; their colors were bright. You wanted to leave your parents' house, Modesta, you were impatient for a house of your own. Months later, the community comes together again to dance around the tree. Gaitán decides to take up the ax once more. *Look, look, don't stop looking*, your mother says, jubilant. The community dances at that never-ending *yunza*. The presents thump to the ground and the tree topples after just one ax blow. The circle dissolves as everyone rushes to gather up something, except you. You stay right where you are, beaming at Gaitán.

○●

You breathe deep the strong scent of Gaitán above you. His neck smells of mountain deer. His chest, of dry earth. Ay, Gaitán, my sweet Gaitán. You put your hand on his back to pull him to you. Closer. Inside, Gaitán moves. It hurts a bit. Ay, you say and pull him toward you again. Ay, and he keeps on moving. His neck, his ears, and his shoulders sweat. A rod of hot iron down there inside you. Gaitán breathes hard. Ay, right there, keep going, it ignites and makes you open your legs wider, Modesta, he keeps on and you shift below him to feel him more. So good, that, there.

Keep going, Gaitán. A vigorous puma running the length of the valley. Inside you, so good, parting you in two. Keep going, Gaitán. Your legs trap him. He thrusts, desperate. Your breasts press against his chest. Split in two, four, a thousand. You tremble, sweat; a moan escapes you. Gaitán navigates your river, which forms a torrent when it surges with his own. Your skin bristles. You tremble in the light of the moon and your body stretches toward the snowcap of the Apu, melting it. Modesta and Gaitán.

○●

Today, they haven't called me up so Romero can ask me his questions. Lying in bed, I look at the ceiling of my cell and remember the day I got married. My husband. Our honeymoon, and his entering me. Right when he entered me, I saw it all. A complete scene. There would come children. A house. A kitchen. Work, too, but add onto it everything else. It jolted me. He jolted in me and thrust inside diapers, plates, kitchen, dress, makeup, over and over and on for evermore. Everything within. It cascaded over me like a landslide. A perfectly staged scene, laid out for me since birth. A path with no exit, the same one that's laid for every woman for having been born thus. My time wrung dry, sand spent from the hourglass, a horse with its eyes blinkered. Keep on going, ask no questions. The only path available to you. I saw it all. Suffocated. I adapted, mounted him. I rode him but there were no reins. The countryside stretched on, could keep stretching on further. But he was still inside me, thrusting. I didn't have the reins. I had to do something.

I shut down, disconnected from that memory. Then I thought about Fernanda, her husband, and the revolution. We had to turn the world upside down, to put it in reverse. The professor explained that the revolution was absolutely necessary, that nothing would change unless forceful measures were carried out with resolve. It had to happen as soon as possible, no wasting a single minute. I wanted to march, too. I did what I could to reconcile domestic life with revolutionary struggle but there wasn't the time. The twenty-four hours of the day weren't enough. Revolution always requires exclusive dedication, an utter and absolute consecration. Having a husband and daughter was holding me back. Impossible to find the right balance. Being a wife was too time consuming. The professor, Fernanda, and I would do great things. He, shining, would be the voice; Fernanda, decisive and strong, would be the arms; and I, focused and visionary, would be the legs. I would go wherever they sent me. When we achieved our main objective and I got to see my daughter again, I would show her the world we'd built. No more hunger, no injustice, no barefoot little children on a patch of sand with no water or schools. Bread on everyone's table. Everyone everyone everyone. We wanted to transform it all.

I sensed the time had come. That night, my husband stretched out in bed. I felt his lips closing in on my neck, initiating the nightly ritual that would drain me of the energy I needed for the revolution. He rolled on top of me, eager, and pushed apart my legs. When I felt his hands moving toward my underwear, I opened my eyes and glared.

"Don't touch me."

Frozen by my voice and my gaze, he left me alone. He avoided my eyes, as if something was scaring him. I took advantage of his hesitation to make my position clear.

"I've got everything ready."

"I didn't think you'd dare," he said, turning his back to me.

"That's exactly your problem, thinking you know me so well."

"And your daughter means nothing to you?"

"She's why I'm leaving. I don't want her growing up in this country the way it is. She'll understand some day."

"Marcela, you're a coward." His voice shrunk as he said that and even seemed to be trembling. Was it fear?

"You're the coward, staying here, nice and comfy on the couch with your newspaper and your television and your little bourgeois life."

"My daughter needs me."

"The revolution needs me."

The next morning, I packed my whole life into a suitcase. After my husband left for work, I took my daughter to my mother's. Everything decided, weighed up, analyzed. There wasn't enough time for me to be a wife. The time had come for me to surrender myself completely.

○●

I erased all marks of weakness. A piece of dampened cotton to wipe the makeup from my face. It had to be clean and pure for this rebirth. Thorough and unconditional subjection. No accessories, earrings, nothing. Hair cut off. Fernanda helped me with that.

She made it match her own; even there, difference would be erased. Equality would begin with us. A simple blouse and blue pants completed my outfit. This was how I would dress to serve the revolution and the party. Utter dedication. Everything for the Guiding Thought. I would be Comrade Marta from that point forward. I joined the party as one joins a religion. My husband left me, expelled from my body. After, to the mountains, to the epicenter. Arm the mind. Train to destroy, get ready to build.

○●

"Mel, you haven't heard the latest! What happened the other day at the club—God, it was so embarrassing."

"What did you do?"

Jimena laughs in her seat beside me while we speed through the city of drizzle on the way to Kraken. Madonna is playing on the radio. I open the window of my SUV and the drizzle wets my face, refreshing me. I light a Marlboro. I tell Jimena to spit it out, we're almost there. Her voice vacillating between uncomfortable and shy, she begins.

"You know how my university is really…well, diverse."

"Diverse?"

"All kinds of people, you know? Not just like you and me."

"Ah…"

"So last week I went clubbing with a girl I study with. I have my democratic side, you know that."

The adjective sounds ridiculous but I bite my tongue to keep from saying so. What are she and I like? Maybe I also give my democratic side a workout taking Jimena to the club because she would never be invited to Ana María's parties.

Jimena goes on to say that when they got there, the sullen bouncer looked her friend over. He made a grimace of annoyance. A bad sign. Jimena quickly grasped what was coming, and understood that the battle was long lost. She turned a half circle, looking at the night sky. *There's a private function tonight*, the bouncer said. Jimena's friend started waving her arms about and raising her voice in protest. *What's wrong with you? We want to go in!* The guy blocked the door with his body, his muscles almost like rocks, a real gym junkie. Jimena started sweating and pleaded, *Please, let's just go.* Her friend stood fast. *I'm telling you, my friend and I want to go in.* The man furrowed his eyebrows and repeated the formula. *There's a private function tonight.*

"I wanted to die, Mel. Wanted the earth to open up and swallow me whole. I was so embarrassed…"

Muscles pulled a disgusted face and stretched his arms toward them in a way her friend didn't like. *What the hell is wrong with you? Get your hands off me!* Jimena, with the most angelic expression of her repertoire and all the strength she was capable of, took her friend by the arm and steered her away from Kraken. Her friend told her off but knew the battle wasn't hers, either.

"But what was the problem? Was she wearing slippers or something?"

"Of course not, she was really nicely dressed, but you know…"
"What?"

"Well, she's really great…It's just that she's a little on the swarthy side…"

Jimena doesn't finish, only manages to laugh. I bite my tongue once more to stop myself from saying how ridiculous her comment sounds, though this doesn't mean it's not amusing. I take another drag of the Marlboro and feel its flavor cushioning my tongue. A dog crosses the street. Where's a dog off to in such a hurry?

"Don't be like that, not getting in can happen to anyone. You know how they are," I say, not entirely believing it myself, exhaling a puff of smoke. Sometimes you make me wish you would disappear, city of drizzle.

"No way, Mel. It would never happen to you. Haven't you seen the way the gorillas at the club treat you? If they don't roll out a red carpet when you show up, it's only because they don't have one."

I don't care about the gorillas and their red carpets, I just want to get there already. I park the car and we head for Kraken. Let's ready our rifles and see what our aim's like tonight. We get in no problem and, before each of us stakes out our portion of the open range of the dance floor, Jimena takes me by the arm to say, "See how we got in? If I'm with you, I'm with God."

"Come on, Jimena," I tell her, "stop being corny, please."

○●

blackout all over the capital it always happens when you got there the lights came back on a tower aha it's not poetry you yourself saw it yes of course what do you want to do now let's go somewhere quieter here it's a scandal I know a place that's open minded perfect *today I pass the time demolishing hotels* you have a beautiful smile sorry but I can't dance I'm with her you said that to a guy

I've come here with you and don't want to dance with anyone else two towers what were you doing alone in a gay disco I like the music and I love dancing But don't you like girls? things aren't always what they seem or slip under the radar *I struggled for freedom but it was never at hand* you haven't said much about yourself all in good time time someday three towers I'll tell you my story time time yes time you know more about me time I don't know where I got the strength to call you it's a good thing you asked me for my number I didn't ask for it you gave it to me *now I'm not calmer but why should I be we all grow up but don't understand* I love the way you dance four towers your eyes are beautiful Melanie sad kind lovely

○●

Each morning you go down to the river to collect water in two soot-blackened pots, Modesta. Your husband and two sons are still asleep, it's very early. Your walk through the ravine is the only time you have to yourself, far from Gaitán's complaints: that there's never enough money, that he's sick of having to travel so often to the other village to sell what your smallholding produces, that lately everything you cook is too salty. Just moan, moan, moan, you're getting so sick of it. That's why you like these hours of the day so much, nice and early, you feel as if you're mistress of the mountains, the birds, the river. Even though they're always changing, you feel like you're mistress of the clouds, too; they look as if they'd fit into the palms of your hands. Light like them, you lie down for a while on the grass and float in your recollections. Where could that red hat be, the one your father gave you?

It suited you so much, and Gaitán would get jealous jealous jealous every time your cousin whistled at you because you looked so good. Your face would turn red in embarrassment, redder than the hat. Gaitán's such a pain when he wants to be. Could he have hidden it from you? What a pest. Mariano is simply your cousin, as if anything would happen with him! Not even if you were crazy. It can't happen between cousins because afterwards, the babies come out strange, with six fingers or even an extra eye. But it's true your cousin is handsome.

Here where you were born, the ground is hard. You sense that life beyond the hills is different. What must it be like over that way? Curiosity still hasn't nested in you enough to give you wings. Its time will come. You collect the water and return home to your family, your lovely little animals, your smallholding. To all those who have a claim on you. This is the land you know and she gives you security; you have deep roots here, you're tied to her even though it takes so much to coax her into producing. Pachamama is plentiful when you treat her right.

You go into the house and the guinea pigs greet you, scurrying about. You've inherited an affection for them from your grandmother. Timid like you, they're shy when they hardly know a person, but settle down and come closer when they start to trust. Killing them saddens you but such is life. Today you smile at the little things, you feed them, pat them, and tomorrow they will be cooked in a big pot, mixed with herbs that smell so good. Tomorrow is your husband's birthday, one of the few times you let yourselves eat the guinea pigs you rear. It costs money to cook them, it most definitely isn't cheap. Wheek wheek wheeeek they squeal during the day, dashing about their pen, and at night their purring blends with your children's breathing.

○●

He gazes at the city through the window overlooking the river. It's a gray day, a typical autumn morning, perfect for sitting on his favorite sofa sipping tea and reading, except that today he has a meeting and a decree to sign. The river below, with its turbid waters, reflects what he encountered when he took office: apathy, lack of vision for the future, stagnation, mediocrity, almost everyone eager to be anywhere but here. People cross the bridge, many of them provincial migrants who have come to the capital to better themselves. They're little stains of the same color; their clothes could almost be confused with the gray sky, all of them dull. He rests his weary gaze on the marble columns of his office.

They arrive, ready to start the meeting. The admiral steps into the office, punctual, his stride firm: this distinction makes him one of the best guests at his parties. Good conversation, good taste, a man of the world. The general seems preoccupied, his steps stiff. He keeps looking at the columns, those pure lines. The others are the ones who speak. *The police are being ambushed time and again. Nowadays, you can't trust anyone. On top of that, the group's leader is in hiding and his only objective is moving forward with what they call the people's war.*

The general spreads a map out over the table. He knows the area; he was there some time ago when the first outbreaks happened. *We must show them that our hands are not going to tremble. They are at war with the State and have to understand who's in charge.*

At this stage of the game words have no effect. The Army must reinforce its bases and the Naval Infantry will take charge of the more tactical matters. Distinguishing between the campesinos who are aligned with the group and those who are not is a difficult undertaking, so we should take forceful measures, as I said earlier. They mark the zones, points on the map. Install bases. That would be war. The police haven't been able to take care of it. He could draw up a plan. A well-organized, methodical plan, a plan that *We cannot develop an intelligence project in detail, it would take too long.* A plan that makes use of intelligence to thwart the enemy, how can you leave aside intelligence? Things need to be thought through. Human lives. *We have to lay waste to wherever subversives are suspected to be present.* Suspected. He puts his hand on the map. It slips and leaves a damp mark on the paper. The entire province stained with sweat. The general and the admiral observe him intently. *They have killed many police officers and there might be more,* one says. *We have to carry out a counterattack,* the other says. He takes his hand off the map. A spiral escaping his grasp. *If we kill thirty, there will surely be a subversive among the dead.* And if there's only one? What about those who are not? *Calculating the number of innocents is not tactical.* Space compresses him. It seems as if the columns are bending. He wants to leave. *We are at war. If we don't contain it now, the violence could spill over and come too close to the capital.*

"Here?"

He sits up straight, nervous. He feels a bead of sweat slipping down his back. He walks toward the window again but no longer sees the river. He knows they're expecting a response from him. The war, here: that can't be. There's so little time until his term ends. He was too passive a few years ago, and now the problem has grown.

Violence is always dangerous, it could lead to an open war. But since we've lacked an iron fist, everything has spun out of control. He thinks about his family and his friends' families. About all those who elected him. He must not let the war get here, whatever the cost. How will they remember him? Will they remember him? Without warning, a ray of sunshine penetrates the heavy cloud cover, causing him to close his eyes. He returns to the table. The sweat stain on the map has evaporated, leaving a wrinkle across the surface. With reluctance, he scribbles down the notes that will become a decree. Authorized. *On your orders, Mr. President.*

○●

how many were there it hardly matters twenty came thirty say those who got away counting is useless crack machete blade a divided chest crack no more milk another one falls machete knife dagger stone sling crack my son crack my sister my wife crack my father crack exposed flesh broken neck machete impaled eyeball bullet femur tibia fibula bullet faceless earless noseless *that's for being terrorists* crack *we're not papacito lindo we're not* don't spit it out don't crack five put them in a line blast in the abdomen bullet blood soup spattering making mud their boots slipping soldier bullet screaming screeching howling burnt bones bullet just ten were enough ropes arms up you stink fetid crack you stink your feet stink their cunts suet machete blow mud the floor chop chop penises testicles for your old mother to eat up open your mouth crack for pity's sake machete blow *put a bullet in them already* crack campesinos machete blow *this is how subversives die* crack lip tooth throat *we're not* bullet *yes you are* ten enough machete blow crack the earth is soaked she can't take more blood crack pachamama vomits the liquid of the people bullet they're escaping bullets they run before more are taken down howling shut up stab eye it won't come out at last you've shut up bitch bullets bullet bullets gust of wind it's finished desolation silence empty pampa they can go back all dead accomarca

○●

How old was I? Maybe twelve or thirteen. I was studying at the nuns' school. I remember they made me read the life of Saint Teresa of Ávila and from that point on I was completely hooked. I was fascinated by that woman: so adventurous, so much grit, a leader who guided and organized other women to reform what had grown outdated. Her one-on-one conversations with the inquisitors and doctors of theology were utterly brilliant. She told them what they wanted to hear; this was how she escaped the bonfire that burned so many other women alive. Her sole, abiding obsession was God. Around that obsession revolved everything else in her life. For Saint Teresa, confinement in the convent was no obstacle to unleashing her reformist plan. I admired her perseverance and camouflage. Her discipline, too. Her clear, fixed and stable center, her upright and solid discipline meant all that was left was to devise the delicate weave of her speech. Say what others want to hear and, in this way, in the shadows, behind what is seen and shown, get to work on one's objectives. Fernanda was right, words could be more powerful than they seemed.

The feminine ferment will be crucial in this struggle, the Leader and Fernanda told me. *The greater the exploitation, the greater one's strength when the time comes to take up arms.* Now it was time for me to be trained, for my body to be disciplined, to transform into a revolutionary weapon. Tougher, more warlike, none of this husband, kitchen, children. Nothing that might weaken me. Increase my strength to put it to the service of the revolution: that was my maxim.

○●

The ravine was muddy after the morning rain. They gave us a few rifles and pistols to train with. My aim was the best of the whole group. I learned to assemble and disassemble the rifle and revolver with my eyes closed, without fail, so fast that my companions wanted to place bets to see how many seconds I took. Body to the ground, running, walking in file, any formation was fit for hitting the target.

From then on I got used to always having a weapon with me. Whereas before I painted on lipstick and felt naked without it, now that the revolutionary struggle had changed my life, I felt naked if I didn't carry my weapon on my belt. My skin had molded to its shape. My hands demanded the revolver I had been assigned to liberate the wounded from their last breath. As if my fingers had lengthened and were injected into the temples of the wretched. Bullet fingers. Gun-barrel arms. Revolver body.

○●

Two days had gone by since the last time we could eat in a village. We had to leave fast when the soldiers showed up. Some comrades fell heroically, but it was impossible to recover their bodies and give them the burials they deserved, wrapped in the party flag. There were only five of us left: Comrade Felipe, three other combatants, and I. We had to meet up with the others.

We knew the soldiers were hot on our trail. We kept making our way through the mountains, but by now my comrades were showing signs of fatigue. No one complained, but the lack of water dried up our will, drop by drop. The way forward got tougher; we had to cut a path through vegetation that seemed put there on purpose to break our spirit. *Let's stop, comrades, please.* One comrade couldn't go on. Comrade Felipe paid no attention to the plea. We were under his command. I noticed that every now and then he turned to look pointedly at me. What could he be thinking? He started singing one of the party songs. We followed along as best we could, but the volume of the singing faded with the light of the day. *Please, Comrade Felipe, let's stop.* Another combatant who could go on no longer. Felipe looked at me. *You decide, Comrade Marta, should we stop or keep on?*

My legs were crying out for rest. My arms were fraying. If only we had just a little water… *We have to lay down our lives for the revolution, Comrade Felipe. We can't afford to waste even a minute. The enemy is afraid and fights mindlessly, but we can't be defeated; we must give our all. Let's keep on!* His eyes shone with respect.

35

○●

"Genuine equality between the sexes can only be realized in the process of the socialist transformation of society as a whole."

MAO TSE TUNG

○●

"Comadre Modesta! How's my godson Abel?"

Justina Quispe shows up, as always, brimming with a joy that floods your house. She has just got back from a brief trip away and comes hauling two flagons of chicha. You greet her with glee. You've known each other since you were little, when you ran after the vicuñas together. As well as dearest friends, Justina is now godmother to your son, which makes the two of you comadres. You tell her about the latest community meeting, when they allotted work to help the Huarotos with their sowing. The husband and wife were both very sick and their children still small, so the whole community was pitching in. The men talked and talked; you were sitting listening to them talk and decide, not once daring to speak up. When the meeting was over, the council had assigned Gaitán more hours than the others because, in his absence, they knew you wouldn't protest.

"Ay, Modesta, I bet Gaitán was furious with you."

"He was, comadre…"

A ball of fury, that's what Gaitán was when he got home that night and you told him how many hours he had to work on the Huarotos' smallholding. He turned fierce, he started raising his voice. He was like a bull. *Learn to make a fuss, learn to be like Dominga, she always speaks up for her husband!* Gaitán grabbed you by the arm and shook you like a rag. *You look silly, all quiet at the council meetings! Why send you there alone!* You withstood your husband's rage and his pushing you about. He dealt you a few blows to the head, really hard, it still hurts.

"What a brute Gaitán is, walloping you like that, comadre, you mustn't let him. Ay, comadre, if it had been me, I'd have pulled his hair and smacked his face."

You tell Justina to calm down. Gaitán is a good man, tough and hardy when it comes to working the land and selling the harvests. What would you do without him? Pachamama doesn't simply fertilize herself, you need your husband's strong arm to coax her into sprouting and nourishing your family. And soon after, the bruises fade. That's just the way it is.

"Gaitán will get what he deserves. He has it coming to him. But for now something else is worrying me."

"What is it, comadre?"

"It's what's in the air, Modesta. No one has seen it coming, but I know it's going to be big trouble, and it's going to hurt us bad."

"Everything is singing it, no? From the little animals to the voices of the rivers and what they're talking about in the marketplace. Everything."

Your comadre stirs the coffee and drops into it some pieces of bread, which float there. She mushes them up in the bottom of the mug.

"We have to prepare for the worst. Now, even with offerings to the Apu, nothing can be done."

"It's as bad as that?"

"Very bad. The Apus have abandoned us. We're being left with nothing."

○●

Sunday morning and all the community members have come to the market loaded with produce. Gaitán has brought along a few hens and some nice fat guinea pigs. A few meters from his stand, the Quechán brothers have brought guinea pigs, too, a lot more than Gaitán's, but none of them as plump. The good-for-nothing Carlos Quechán, all ungainly with oily hair and an idiotic expression, comes over. Gaitán prefers not to give him the time of day but his blood boils when he sees Carlos strutting about before him as if he were king of the world. He thinks he's all that because his father is governor. *Who does this fool think he is?* Gaitán wonders, and he packs some coca leaves into his mouth after the appropriate offering to the Apu.

Carlos Quechán inspects Gaitán's guinea pigs.

"If you're buying, they're really expensive, eh! You couldn't afford them."

"Ha! Gaitán, you're such a wit! Mine are far superior, you'll see how they sell."

Close to midday, the market is at its liveliest. People from all over come with news from the nearby villages. Some say the new president is going to build a road to connect all of you to the provincial capital and open a few health posts, but it still hasn't been decided which hamlets will be the lucky ones. *Around here, the crying baby gets the milk, papacitos.* Others say that the terrorists are moving further and further into the province and setting up schools to teach their ideas. *They're welcome if they're giving away cows. They say they steal them. Best they go to another village, then. They're nothing but cattle rustlers.* The human surge flows over the plaza through the smell of vegetables and animals. The dogs lie in wait by the bird stalls to see if luck will have it that a bit of innards is thrown their way. *Manuela told me that if you don't give them your animals, they treat you real bad. I've heard they kill. The southern communities are going to ask the army to install bases to protect them.* People walk among the corncobs, the potatoes, the substantial sweet potatoes, stalls bursting with hens and their eggs. A knot of shouting butchers almost deafens that side of the market. *The police are no use against them. Over in the other hamlet the police escaped, fleeing like deer, when they saw the terrorists coming down the hill. The soldiers, on the other hand, can take them on. They're better prepared.*

"Have a listen, they're talking to you," Gaitán says to Carlos when he sells another wheeking guinea pig. He has only two left.

"Go choke on your coca leaf, Gaitán. That's all *you* know how to do, whine when they give you too much work with the Huarotos, you lazy shit. No wonder Modesta's had enough of you already," Carlos spits on the ground, not looking at him.

"Says he who doesn't even have a dog to keep him company! I'm almost done selling my guinea pigs, and you've still got a whole box full, you lousy git."

An elderly blind man rattles his tin to see if they remember that he needs to eat, too. *Let's form a group of representatives to go ask for a health post. Let's get some cows together in case the rustlers show up in the village.* Two chicha sellers sing, animated, accompanying their patrons, whose cheeks flush from the drink. *I'm not giving my precious cows to anyone. The soldiers should come, we should propose that to the governor.* Gaitán has just sold his last two guinea pigs and picks up the coarse cotton cloth he had spread out on the ground.

Over in the hamlets further up they say the Sinchi soldiers laid waste to the terrorists. They give it to them hard. I'm with you, let them come take care of the insurgents. Carlos Quechán continues to eat his lunch unhurriedly, looking, bored, at the buyers who pass by his stall.

"Bye, you lousy git," Gaitán says.

Carlos doesn't look at him. He gulps down the piece of potato he has in his throat and curses Gaitán from the depths of his soul. *May the air stick in your lungs and the Pishtaco suck you dry.* If it weren't for the fact that his father would demand an explanation, he would grab a guinea pig and twist its foot, holding its head down so it couldn't bite. *Disgusting animals.*

○●

"They just don't know their place, these journalists," says someone in a certain office, snorting, shaking his head disapprovingly.

"What does the article say?"

"Listen to this: 'Unidentified elements have attacked the settlement of V***. They stole food from community members and threatened them with rifles. No one resisted. Once they had gathered up the food, they took animals. They left a red flag, which was kept by the inhabitants.' Afterwards, all the usual, it even seems as if they've copied the other article."

"Pass that over here. Watch and learn." He takes his pen and strikes out the phrase "unidentified elements" and replaces it with "Shining Path elements." He looks over the subsequent lines and crosses out "red flag" to write instead "red rag."

"There we go. Now it can be handed over to the newsreader."

○●

I get a call from a reporter who has just got back from the central conflict zone. Usually he has a calming, unwavering air, but today he is annoyed, irritable. His voice is almost enough to make the receiver tremble. I sense he's being careful not to shout but can't help raising his voice. *They've never edited a story of mine in such an outrageous way. Not ever, Mel. It looks like orders from higher up...* They smudge the blood on the paper so it won't spatter the city of drizzle. It has already spattered, even if they don't want to see it. National security, they argue.

I light a Marlboro and, while the nicotine activates my nerve centers, the enraged journalist tells me what he saw on his last visit and everything he had included in the story he filed. *It's hell up there. They're overdoing it.* We have to free ourselves from words on paper. It will have to be images that show the situation as it really is. From its position on the table, my camera observes me. I grasp it in my left hand with an ease that comes from so many shots and framings. It's clear to me that our next trip will be to Ayacucho. *But it's so dangerous, Melanie, anything could happen to you. You're too young to put your life at risk.* I have to shoot at reality to trap it in my lens, to turn it into images. My twenty-five years are no obstacle: on the contrary, they're sheer energy. *It's hard to get there, there are almost no means of transport.* We can't let the facts get lost; they have to be recorded. *It's really dangerous, even more so if you're a woman.* Certainly there are few of us in the minefield that is our profession. I know thousands of anecdotes that don't bear repeating. I'd prefer to end the conversation here.

The night wears on with a placidness I'm keen to shake off. To dance—curfew or no curfew. To dance before heading to the mountains. Let music explode in my body before any bomb.

○●

The music thuds all throughout the house. Tonight, few women are dancing at Ana María's. Instead, they hang on each other's words. The news is almost the same, some know a few more details. Someone looks for me, apprehensive. *Is it true you're going there?* When did these women find out? I can't confirm it but I don't want to deny it, either. *To the mountains? Right now? Have you forgotten what they did to those reporters in Uchuraccay?* It's years since that happened. *Those campesinos get the wrong idea, you know. Be careful, Mel.* I hate being here. We have to break the circuit of censorship and the monopoly over information. No doubt some understanding has been reached with the government. They're controlling everything. One of the women suddenly becomes interested in the conversation. *Campesinos? They're the worst. My father was stripped of his land because of that absurd Agrarian Reform. And what happened? Go ask them. Go see how they've let everything go to waste.* Now's not the time to put things into historical perspective or talk about inequality. If I bring back images, might these women be able to see something different? Might they truly see? *Those insurgents are doing us a favor. I hope they keep getting rid of them. They'd do well to wipe them all out.* The woman who says this has become tangled in an attack of laughter; clearly she's had too much to drink. And if they killed your siblings? I want a vodka.

I prefer to distance myself from them a bit. I'm fed up with the things they say, but I need them. *I'll do what I can, Mel, I'll speak to my father, I'm sure he will lend you a hand.* A friend opens doors in such circumstances. *They'll give you the safe-conduct in no time and maybe even an escort.* The path cleared to the mountains. But I don't want an escort. I want more music, want to dance. I play with the cherry and ice in my vodka lime. I make myself comfortable on the sofa. It's been a few weeks since Daniela went back to Paris and who knows when she'll be back. Assuming she does come back. And if she doesn't, the world will keep on turning, as always. Perhaps it was a mistake to speak to her again. *Are you insane, Mel? Traveling there at this point means going into the mouth of hell.* Pure metaphors…

○●

thud thud thud you dance I dance alone together she leads me to the corner can't resist your perfume she says your perfume your smile your eyes your hands she says my mouth my lips my tongue a frenzied animal thud thud thud lights laser lights beat beat *bandit lover friend* she hangs from my neck stay there I'm getting wet lights down down down now yes *torment love the tide* yes *heart captive lover* yes I don't want to see your face *without mystery* down bury yourself there down sink your face *bandit bandit* you say something no follow the electricity again my giddy center my back an arch *hurricane hurricane* held breath your damp face who are you *I will get lost in a moment with you* thud my number? thud *forever* clean your face thud what planet do you live on

○●

I remember the night in detail because the next morning I was to return to the field. I had to take reinforcements to our combatants in the mountains. The time had come; I crept toward Comrade Leader and Fernanda's bedroom. The half-shut door beckoned. I remember everything as if I'm seeing it right now. My pupils dilating, tensing like my muscles down below, beating, desiring, eyes watering, dampening, fixed on their skin. On the Leader's skin. On Fernanda's skin. My pupils opening and closing, my longing sex opening and closing. My panting taking on a slow, deliberate rhythm, beads of pleasure in each breath. Not much variation. Militant in their rhythm. Mostly he on top of her. He thrusts and exhales deep. The hierarchy maintained at this time of night. I don't need to touch them to be part of them. I graze their bodies with my eyes. I know they feel it. I know they feel my gaze on their backs, my eyes on their skin.

I have to control the pain in my center, absorb it until it disappears and dissipates in a vapor without weight or consequence. Dominate my flesh, my eyes, their skin. The body itself does not exist. What exists is a forceful act. A retaliation from the State. A gestating woman. Pieces of an informer. Bits of a traitor. There are also (they always say) massacres. Devastation. Quotas. Papers, letters, one atop the other, mounting with excessive order. Discipline exists. The word exists but doesn't hurt. It cuts, but doesn't hurt. Kills, but doesn't hurt. Genocidal explosion. Hammer and sickle. The red sun. The dawn.

○●

"There's something we're still not entirely clear about, teacher," Major Romero pushes back a curl that falls across his forehead. His ever-present cigarette starts to fill the small room with smoke.

"Since you've had us locked up, nothing is clear to me either, Major."

"That's why we're here, to clear things up. It looks as though you really enjoyed filming yourselves, is that right?"

"Our historic actions need to be preserved for future generations."

"If you say so, teacher. One video in particular caught my attention, Comrade Two's funeral. What did she die of?"

He always comes back to the same thing. The night of the funeral, we all sang a song to her memory. Comrade Leader led the tribute. *A shining example of giving one's life for the party and the revolution. A beautiful torrent of your blood has irrigated our revolution.* Her blood was needed if we were to keep advancing along the shining revolutionary path.

A few weeks before, dissent had arisen. Comrade Leader wanted to move the armed struggle to the city, where the entire leadership was now located. Fernanda wanted to keep it in the countryside. She quoted Engels: "Movement is itself a contradiction." Dialectics that left the party tangled up. I witnessed the dialectic struggle. Comrade Two was perhaps forgetting our pact of subjection to Comrade Leader. "Absolute subjection to the leadership, my total, full, thorough, unconditional support for the most illustrious son of the class. My subjection to him who runs the People's War in Peru, the shining beacon of world revolution. My full subjection to the party, my full subjection to our general political line, my full subjection to our unconquered understanding of Marxism-

Leninism-Maoism Guiding Thought." Comrade Three was smart enough to keep silent. Fernanda forgot she was Comrade Two, subject to the party and the Leader. How could she forget that? Where was her head? Comrade Leader wanted to act as soon as possible in the capital, the seat of the State, whose ravenous politics had to be annihilated. He looked at her and repeated Mao's phrase: "Unless you enter the tiger's den, how can you catch the cubs?" I found out that, from then on, his meetings with Comrade Three became more frequent, until I got the message to return to the capital for Fernanda's funeral.

"Comrade Two suffered a heart attack."

"A heart attack?" Romero scratches his head, shaking it incredulously. "And now, teacher, who would you have me believe?"

"Me, of course, Major, who else?"

"I'm confused. You tell me she suffered a heart attack. Your Leader has told us she died in combat. And two other commissars give me different versions: suicide and falling down the stairs. I have a few options to choose from."

We can't contradict ourselves. Does raking these things over achieve anything? I won't say any more about Fernanda. She had to abide by party rules, she knew that was how it had to be. If Romero has spoken to our Leader it means they've kept him alive. That's what's important.

○●

Our contact has shown up at last; he's going to guide us in the conflict zone. He seems like a savvy, astute individual: good qualities for this profession. *There are rumors going around, señorita. You have to keep your eyes and ears well open, like this.* He widens his eyes as if he's about to devour us. Very serious. He is small, compact and solid, and moves with agility when he follows us to the car. They have assigned us an escort of two soldiers. Protection or control? One of them carries a walkie-talkie so that we have permanent contact with the military base. In this city, all activities seem to be carrying on as usual. Some walls, marked in red, shout Shining Path rallying cries. *Going to the villages would be of greater interest. An hour's car ride from here, there's a hamlet where they say strange elements made an incursion.* The compact man smiles wryly when he says "strange elements." He has won my confidence. We keep on, my colleague Álvaro grasping his video camera more tightly than usual, the greenish veins in his hands visible. His eyes are on the road ahead as if he wants to impose a veil of silence.

The small main square welcomes us with its simplicity. Poverty is visible in the paint chips that flake off the house walls. We get out of the military jeep. The other soldier accompanying us is dressed as a civilian; he says it's to avoid suspicion. I wonder from who and toward who. We are journalists: why would anyone be suspicious? Our guide has a good rapport with the people. *You have to be patient. Little by little, gain their confidence. Talk to them, invite them to eat, accept what they offer because, if not, they'll be offended and you'll lose any ground already gained.* We've arrived here after lunch. While it's quite cold, the air is calm. A muddy ball checkered with patches tumbles into sight, almost mowing down a pair of hens that are pecking mechanically at the skeleton of a corncob. Three children hurry toward us. A woman I assume is the mother of one of them, or maybe all of them, rounds the hens up and tries to herd them toward a coop a few meters away. Plaits, a felt hat, and—there it is—a smile. I've got her. In that smiling instant, I've captured her. I'd like to keep photographing her but my shot has robbed her of that smile and she has run off to shut herself in the house, forgetting the hens.

Our guide takes coca leaves and pisco to where one of his contacts lives. A middle-aged couple opens the door. I see they are apprehensive. At first they don't want to talk. We chew the coca and all start to relax a little. Álvaro turns on the video camera. *The subversives are like devils, that's what the priest tells us, mamacha.* The husband takes a long swallow of pisco. He narrows his eyes and the alcohol makes him shudder, but he quickly takes another, longer swig. *The reason they don't get hungry is because they feast on human flesh, the liver, the lungs; they drink blood, that's what we've heard.* Both their bodies stiffen when he utters that description. The man keeps talking, hardly pausing long enough to gulp down another mouthful. *Those wretches barely reach the village before they start robbing everything in sight. If you don't give it to me I'll kill you—saying things like that. They kill the children or spirit them off to the mountain. They killed a friend of mine because he wouldn't let others take their sheep to pasture on his fields. It was his land, it was his right to refuse, wasn't it? The terrorists asked who the miserable miser was, the one who didn't share his property, and went to find him. They opened his neck up with a knife.* He stops and looks at the floor. I'm finding it a bit difficult to move my tongue because the coca has numbed it. His wife puts a hand on his knee. I freeze them when a tear starts forming, making her eyes shine. Only she reacts, averting her gaze.

He keeps drinking and talking. *They're robbing us of everything: cows, hens, two mules we had.* He starts to cry. *If they take my children I don't know what we'll do and if they keep stealing from us, how on earth am I going to feed them?* Why didn't you report them to the police? *They always come back, señorita. If you want to survive, you have no choice but to cooperate with them. A friend of mine heard that if the terrorists find out you've spoken to the police, they kill you on the spot. They always know. They find out everything. One thousand, that's how many eyes they say those devils have.* His voice is heavy with impotence. Tears still moisten his face. *That's why the priest says they're demons, mamacha,* the wife interjects. I notice she has something strange hanging from her neck. Its form is familiar, but at the same time hard to define. Is that a fingernail at its base? *We have to pray because those devils can come back any one of these nights to kill us. That's why we pray every day, and we fast, too, so God will save us. Nights here are dangerous. Best hurry back to wherever you came from.*

They won't say anything further. We thank them for having us in their home and leave. Álvaro has said nothing all afternoon.

○●

It is colder now. Our guide, who every time I look at him seems even more like a bad copy of a spectacled bear, takes us to another house. *They use them as amulets,* one of the soldiers says to me, *they dry them and hang them around their neck to ward off betrayal. That's what they say the fingers are for.* I had already heard something about such amulets. The journalist who was censured mentioned he'd seen a few dead bodies missing index fingers. He'd said it was becoming fairly common.

The guide says he doesn't believe in those superstitions. He adjusts his glasses to give himself a more serious air. He starts to tell me about his career and the many journalists he has accompanied in the area, but my attention is drawn to two women approaching along the same path. One is young; her black felt hat and two plaits frame her face perfectly. Her eyebrows are furrowed with tension, and in her eyes there's fear, mistrust, and rage. An elderly woman walks beside her, carrying a small girl on her shoulders. The elderly woman is bony and avoids looking me in the eye. Her lips are moving slightly as if she is repeating a useless litany. Both have their fists clenched. The girl turns to look at me when I click the shutter release. *Papacitos, the military came through here and carried off some community members, saying they were terrorists. They're not, papacitos, they're not.* The soldier regards her with an icy serenity. They know all about amulets and torture. The looks exchanged are like arrows. *Or it's also possible that's not what I saw, señores. I'm not sure. Ay, I know nothing. Best you don't write down any of what I just said. I don't understand what I see, not even what my hands feel. My memory's failing. I'm probably imagining things.* She twists her fist with even greater force, and anger draws her eyebrows closer together.

Mamacha, please, now that you're going to the capital, please take my daughter, they'll kill her here. Take her to the capital, please. I have relatives there. Please leave her with them. She insists so much that I can't say no. There are strange ways of saving a life. We decide not to pay any more visits this afternoon and to get going right away.

The girl has been asleep the whole trip. *At this rate, your maternal instinct will kick in and I don't want to be around when that happens,* Álvaro jokes, the first time in the whole journey. There's still so much to uncover, to photograph. I have to go back.

○●

The women advance, marching along the gray patio. The first of them holds a banner with the image of Comrade Leader. *Honor and glory to the proletariat and the people of Peru.* Hair trained under green caps. Red blouses. Aquamarine skirts to the knee. Marching in formation. Educated in the shining trenches of combat. Jail, others call it; prison. All at the same pace. *Give one's life for the party and the revolution.* Banners of red flags with a yellow star. Torches in hand. Rhythm. Rhythm. Rhythm. Drum one. Drum two. Drum three. The feminine ferment, rising. *We travel a shining path. We shall struggle without truce to the end.* Leg up. Leg down. Leg up. *People's revolution.* Leg down. *Communism.* Gazes raised to the walls with their enormous murals, from which Mao, Lenin, Marx, and our Leader look down on them. They are in jail to learn. *Armed struggle against hunger. We will vanquish vile imperialism. Victory is in the hands of the people and their firearms. Women's* says one side *women's* responds the other *movement* says one side *movement* responds the other. *Women's popular movement* all together. Again. *Women's* says one side *women's* responds the other *movement* says one side *movement* responds the other. *Women's popular movement* all together. They organize themselves in columns. Posing as if in a Chinese mural. Tai chi step. *The great helmsman.* They keep time. One two one two one two one two.

○●

It is the same room as always, down through the years of the life of the republic. But now it's someone else. He also looks toward the river. He has never paid the columns any attention. Recalling the news irritates him. He moves away from the window and goes to the mirror to check his reflection. His shirt collar fits him perfectly. The blue suit does, too. He is sweating a bit. He senses lunchtime approaching. His stomach announces it. He dreams of that *seco de chabelo* the presidential chef has promised him.

The general arrives at last. It is preferable to settle the matter at once. It's not as if he's at a public gathering where he can expound for hours and hours, feeling the vibration of the roaring multitude following his words in a hypnotic trance. In these meetings he can be more concise. More sparing. As soon as the general takes a breath to interject, he cuts him off. He speaks almost mechanically about the situation in the jails. Subversives and jails. Do they go there to reform or to come out more convinced of their ideology? There are things that simply cannot be permitted. They even have a little school. What's happened to law and order, then. A firm hand so they understand. It will be up to the general to assume responsibility, as corresponds with his rank. Each of us triumphs where possible, do we not?

He notes that the general is impatient when he moves his arms with a certain discomfort on the table. *Mr. President, I await your orders.* He prefers not to sit down, and instead returns to the window. Hunger. He wants it to be over and done with. To get a move on. The slow pace of others irritates him, as it does when they fail to understand the first time, when he has to repeat everything all over again.

You need to take action in the jails. He tells the general that he may leave. He should not expect memos, or decrees, because there will be none.

○●

When your father Samuel got an idea in his head, there was no talking him out of it, Modesta. A little girl, you were. Your mamá had cooked his favorite dish to see if that might butter him up. *We need to send her to school.* But he didn't want to. What for. She should see to the smallholding, or learn to weave. When she marries, her husband will take care of everything. *So she can hold her own in life. It's her turn. So she can learn to read.* The more your mamá spoke to him, the more stubborn he got. She should learn to cook, why all this reading and writing. He scraped the plate of its last crumb. *You're so stubborn.* He didn't want to know any more about it. You heard everything and kept quiet. She winked at you and smiled.

After your papá left to work the field, your mamá showed you one of your older brother's books. *My daughter, look at the letters. Your brother copies them down, here in his exercise book, and this is how he learns to read and write.* She left the book and showed you a table of colors. *This is the alphabet table, look, I memorized the letters like this. Don't tell your papá because he'll get angry.* The table had a figure for each letter. The one that said A looked like a bent iron. The B was like handles of the coffee cup. The C was in the form of the moon when it was waxing. You were enjoying this reading business. *Take this new little exercise book I bought for you. Grip the pencil like this, look.* Your mamá took your hand and you drew your first A.

You smiled, victorious. There were a lot of blank pages, white waiting for letters. *I'm going to teach you all I can, my daughter,* she told you, stroking your forehead.

○●

I wanted to see it. Time and again the nuns at school repeated, *You don't look, girls, and you don't touch.* I could no longer restrain my curiosity, so, dispelling my sense of shame, I lay on the bed after taking a bath. How old must I have been? Twelve, maybe. I was completely naked. The softness of the quilt embraced me. I was tempted to touch myself, to feel the electricity, but this time I wanted to see it first. I had by my side the mirror, a big one, about the size of the cover of a photograph album, as if it were a picture frame. I separated my legs and put the mirror between them. I took a breath. I would finally see it. Would I see it? Better not. Was it not enough to feel it and know it was there and could give pleasure even though the best way to gain entrance into heaven was to avoid it? No. I had to see it. I wanted to see it. How embarrassing! I'd had it for twelve years and until that moment I didn't know what it was like. I pushed myself up on my elbows. I peered at myself. Some hairs. Now, to separate them. I held the mirror in my left hand and with the fingers of my right parted the curtain of hair. There it was. I looked at it. I narrowed my eyes to make it out better. There it was. That little cowl must be where the fingers slipped to produce the electrical current. My index and middle fingers made an inverted V to expose it. It looked like a broad bean parted down the middle. "Dicotyledonous group."

Those must be the lips. All of it somewhere between red, purple, and pink. I peered at the opening. A baby's head passes through there? How horrifying. I enlarged the V a little more to look at it in detail. "Let's see. Don't let it transcend outward, and think as if it's not being listened to, and chrome and not be seen." The hairs beginning at the edges. Disgusting. It seemed to me such an ugly thing...

○●

A thousand eyes and a thousand ears. It is monstrous and unfathomable, just like God. It hears and sees everywhere, in every direction. One eye is called word. One ear is called word. The other eye: word. And the other ear? The same, on and on, for all the two thousand organs that are everywhere. My body multiplies in this way not in the organs but in the word. I see, feel, hear, know, and experience because they understand that's where the only trinity, the central committee, the light of the path is to be found. Placing an eye-word in a suitable place is a more delicate task than planting a grenade and detonating it, more delicate than calculating the exact quantity of dynamite and ANFO in a car bomb. The effects even more explosive, more potent, more prolonged. If they think a body blown into hundreds of pieces is impressive, it means they haven't understood a thing. A thousand eyes and a thousand ears. Like God. Everywhere. I wanted to be God.

○●

Your husband left two days ago to visit relatives and wouldn't be back for three weeks. He would probably stay a little longer to see if someone would purchase part of the harvest in advance. You have Enrique in your arms when the terrorists burst into the communal room. Two of your own are thrown against the wall and struck with rifle butts. Justina Quispe is not intimidated. *Opportunist faggot dogs!* It would have been better if she'd kept quiet. Nice and quiet like you, Modesta. *You're only ruthless because you've got guns.* Two men grab her and carry her out of the room. They strip her naked and hang her by her plaits from the flagpole, just as another time they left five dogs with their throats slit, hanging by their front paws. Justina screams uncontrollably, insulting and cursing them. One of the subversives—Felipe, you hear him called—his face rigid and expressionless, pushes the blade of his dagger against the throat of your comadre Justina. Pachamama is fertilized with her blood. *That's how those who don't respect the revolution die.* And he sheaths the dagger in his boot, storing there a cry that everyone represses.

They drag Fabián Misaico, community councilor, to the middle of the room. They slip a rope around his neck and with one strike of the rifle butt fell him to his knees. Fabián is dealt one blow after the other to the face. He almost can't make anything out; his eyes are swollen. A flow of blood spills from his left eyebrow, another from his bottom lip, yet another from his left cheek. A suffering Christ with no crown. His wife, Dominga, lets out a wail that pierces the room. *Don't kill my dear husband!* One of the terrorists, huge and with the footfalls of a jaguar, moves toward her and then drags her over to where Fabián lies. *We were waiting for you. You're going to help us install the government of the people. Stab him! Stab this traitor!* And he holds out the dagger to Dominga. *How can I stab him, señor, when he's my husband? I can't, señor, I can't.* The man grows enraged, hoarse and furious as a bull. *Stick it into him, for fuck's sake!* Dominga is gentle as a fawn. The bull bellows and Dominga does not stop crying out *He's my husband!* The dagger, wrapped by force in Dominga's hand, plunges into Fabián Misaico's heart. The revolution has reached your community.

Your son Enrique starts to bawl, breaking the silence that weighs heavy in the wake of Fabián's death. Felipe raises an eyebrow. He's a predatory condor, irritated by the little one's uncontrollable crying. He tells you to press him to your chest. You refuse; you're not about to suffocate your own son. *Either you press him against your chest or what I'll do is this* and in the air he makes out as if he is putting something facedown and tearing it in half like a piece of paper.

You know you would never suffocate your own son, but little Enrique is no longer with us.

○●

Every day, at exactly four in the afternoon, new words parade into your ears just like the terrorists parade every morning. That if the class, they say, that if the proletariat, they say, that if the revolution, they say, that if the people's war, they say, are saying, say. You only nod in agreement, already tuning out. They speak of people you don't know, a certain Marx, a certain Lenin, a certain Mao, and a certain President Leader who is the boss of them all. We're all going to be equal, they say. They sound just like the politicians who have passed so often through the community, but these ones already have their president. President of where, you wonder. The engineer was the president of the nation, you remembered that clearly. Their leader was president, then, of where exactly? You wanted to walk up to your smallholding with your beloved animals and get away from it all for a few minutes. Even just to take a little drink to the Apu so he won't forget you.

You sense that all eyes are on you. You ask them to repeat the question. *The struggle is long and there's no time for daydreaming,* they say, and pull you up to the front by your plaits. Your hat falls off. *Don't hurt me, papacito, please,* you beg, clasping your hands together. The other one has fire in his eyes and in his tongue. *Kneel.* You think of your comadre Justina, the chicken you'll cook for lunch, your husband and Abel, the one son you have left. Where has Gaitán got to? *Have mercy, papacito. I won't get distracted again.* When he has got you to kneel down, he steps on your right calf, immobilizing you, and with ten lashes opens up wounds down your back. You burn all over. A few drops slip down your blouse but don't reach the floor. *Forgive me, papacito, forgive me.*
The man releases your leg and brings his face to your ear. His metallic voice scrapes your trembling eardrums and he makes you repeat the slogan, say it, repeat it, name them. It is his voice, not yours, though the air propelling that voice comes from your lungs and makes your vocal cords vibrate in a cry that is not your own: *Long live the party!*

○●

A plate of food; it is no trouble to dish up a plate of food, Modesta. You are always the one who nourishes, who provides. Whoever comes to your table will be welcomed, always, because you are the provider, tending to others, like the earth in which your generous broad beans, your silky-bearded corn, and your rock-shaped potatoes grow. Animals are made for sating man's hunger. The terrorists have asked for lunch, so you set about gathering together what's needed; you have to fix them something to eat. A little hen that was poor Justina's. You cook it quick smart, otherwise you might be next. You cut into its neck with a blade. Just like they did to Justina. You want to cry but squeeze your eyes shut and breathe deeply. You offer some coca leaves to the Apu and then stuff them into your mouth. You don't want to end up at the bottom of the ravine like half your community. You need to keep yourself alive because you're all little Abel has left. The coca leaf is bitter; you swallow down the saliva and cry with your mouth numb. The hen has stopped kicking.

○●

"How many what?"

"You heard me right, Mel, I asked how many centimeters of film you want."

"Now I have to measure my work by the centimeter?"

"Those are the new rules, there's no money for imported material and everything's being rationed. Film, travel allowance, everything."

"Then however many centimeters five of the usual rolls of film adds up to. You do the math, honey."

He starts grumbling. How many centimeters are needed to depict everything? Will a centimeter of film be enough for the dead body of one adult? Half a centimeter if it's a child? And a whole village? Cruelty by the centimeter.

○●

The soldier escorts encumber our reporting. On this trip, we'll have to do without them. The campesinos are increasingly wary and tense up when they see them. If the soldiers come dressed as civilians, they recognize them because of their haircuts and the way they walk. They're impossible to camouflage.

They look so content seated at the mess. Two of the soldiers have brought back a goat, they probably confiscated it from some small-holding close by. Some steal, they steal, the others steal, everyone doing their best to survive. *A bit of meat, finally! We were so sick of living on rice and potatoes!* They share out helpings for us, too. Most of them are young, still beardless—sons of campesinos, campesinos themselves. The one whose gaze had frozen the poor woman on our last trip laughs with his companions now, showing perfect teeth, the canines a tad sharp. *It's so long since I've seen my family, señorita, I've been here far too long, have seen so many terrifying things.* The smoke of the roasted meat envelops them, shielding them from the war for a few minutes. They're like a group of adolescents telling each other about their pranks, flings, missing their own. One of the officials stops eating. He looks at me.

You're all too lucky, you are. I don't know how you got a safe-conduct, they're not giving them out just like that. Even my superiors have made it known that we need to look out for you. I think about the vodka and those women. Cheers to them, whose names I can't say, who I also have to protect. I smile at the captain, not saying anything in particular. My smile makes him a bit uncomfortable; he tightens his grip on his plate and moves toward the soldiers, turning his back on us. The volume of the group's conversation rises. More stories, some laughs, all enveloped in that meat smoke.

○●

Now's our chance. Álvaro, our guide and I move away as if heading out for a stroll. Bit by bit, we manage to leave behind the watchful eyes. We find some transport. I want to go where other journalists haven't been yet. Our plan works: three hours later, we're far from the escorts in a hamlet that seems almost deserted. Each hamlet has fewer people than the last, whether because of forced or voluntary displacement, I'm not sure. Along the way, we come across a woman. She is alone, hurrying; there is a lost look in her eyes and her chin is trembling. She eyes us warily. Our guide approaches and manages to get a few words out of her. *Everyone is afraid of their neighbors. Nowhere is safe, papacito. No one knows whether a relative might be a terrorist, too.* Something has cracked, here. We tell her she can get in and we'll drive her home. *No, papacitos, there's almost no one left in the hamlet.* When we ask her what happened and why she's walking alone, she squeezes my hand. Hers is cold and sweaty. She doesn't want to answer.

She is shaking all over. We let her go and continue on to the
hamlet. What will become of her?

The atmosphere grows strained, and a faint cloud brushes
against the windscreen. And with that, there is an intense odor,
spicy at first, then acrid, something new but not really. We're a few
meters from the plaza and there are a number of places where
bonfires are smoking. The stench becomes unbearable. Something
scorched or rotten. Nausea.

"Let's get out of here."

Was it Álvaro who said that? Did I? We turn on our heel at
the same time. After what I've seen, I don't want to be in this
place any longer. But our guide doesn't want to come with
us. He has relatives in this hamlet and wants to see how they
are. He sketches us a map with directions on a piece of paper
smudged with mud. *Follow this track and when you get to these
parts here, tell the locals I sent you. They'll be good to you, and you
might be able to get more footage for another story. Here's hoping the
situation there is better. Good luck. Hopefully we'll see each other in
the city tomorrow.* Álvaro and I get in the car and put some distance between that repulsive stench and us. We couldn't look.
The hamlet where we left our guide doesn't hang about us as an
image, but as a smell, which has seeped into every pore of our
bodies. That smell. Branded in our memory.

○●

The next hamlet is a cloud of smoke. It's hard to make out anything clearly. My camera feels heavier than usual. That's fine;

its weight anchors me to reality in this spectral place. What's left when everything is done? Nothing. Where should I go look now? What will my lens focus on? We proceed nervously— we've already had a taste of what we might come across— but each time is as if it's the first. I will never be able to say I saw it all. There's always something more terrible a few steps away. Horror can always grow, expanding through every particle of air. When the smoke dispels, I'll click away at the shutter release once more, capturing the shots, my hand will guide the camera—or will the opposite be true? The perfect frame to show—show who? What for? Sometimes I'd rather not look, I wish the camera would bear sole witness. The frame will shout what is sooner stifled. I can't believe it, that smell, again. The smell. The silence. The smell and the silence cling to the composition here and now. What does it mean to look? How can I make that smell impregnate the photo? A thousand shots are not enough for me. Kilometers of film are not enough. But there the story is, in front of my camera. May eyes smell all this and feel the smoke clearing to reveal what I want and don't want to keep on seeing. May my camera see it.

When we get out of the car, the wind wraps awkward arms around us. It weaves a silence that doesn't fit with the time of day. A dog emerges from the smoke and comes up to us, sniffing. Sweet little thing. Seeing a dog used to make me happy, but here they bring grim tidings. The silence, the wind, and the dog form a heartbreaking triad. With cameras at the ready, we keep on until the haze dissipates and two dead bodies bid us welcome to the hamlet. The smell of melted skin assaults us.

Álvaro moves toward the woman. *It was a shot to the head.* The woman is young, twenty-something, my age or maybe younger. By her side is the body of a man. Nothing is left of his face. It's a mass devoured by the dogs, maybe by the one that greeted us, though there are others howling in the distance.

○●

"Face mutilated, face covered, face closed, this man, nevertheless, is whole and lacks nothing. He has no eyes and he sees and cries. He has no nose and he smells and breathes. He has no ears and he listens. He has no mouth and he talks and smiles."

CÉSAR VALLEJO

○●

Surrounded by these white walls, while I wait for Major Romero, sometimes I'm caught off guard by a man whose death I speeded up. I remember his eyes. They've stuck in my mind. His eyes implored me not to finish him off. I hesitated. It was so brief that no one noticed. It would have cost me my position in the party. His eyes asked me not to do it. I had to make my face a mask of ruthlessness. I had given up so much for the revolution that a pair of eyes wasn't going to distance me from my objective.

A coup de grâce, they call it. A coup de gracias, I called it. It wasn't in cold blood, it was simply the final act of the play, the instant his life came to an end. Some were just about dead when I delivered the final bullet. They seemed almost grateful that

I would end their suffering. But this time it was different. Those eyes spoke from a body that felt almost no pain. If it hadn't been for my bullet, he would have lived on. But that's how it is; the revolution demands its share of blood. That's how it is. I battle that memory and think about my childhood. I have to unstick those eyes from my mind.

○●

"Marcela, darling, what's all this?"

I still remember my mother's voice repeating my old name. Marcela. The table was covered with a spotless white cloth; I had put a great Bible on top of it, the largest in the house, bound in black leather with a reddish cross on the cover and edged in gold. An empty wine glass covered in shiny paper sat in the middle of the table. To one side was a small pan also covered in silver paper. Inside there were a few white pieces of cardboard cut into circles, maybe six or seven. Another large, circular piece of white cardboard rested beside the pan. To the left of the table were two perfectly clean bottles, their labels removed, one full of water and the other, red wine.

"I'm celebrating mass, mamá..."

That's what I said, deeply solemn. She smiled and called my sister, Rosa, to explain a few things to me. She taught the catechism, dedicated her time to the youth missionaries. I adored my sister; I would have done anything she asked of me. With just one look, she understood everything. She saw it was an altar and I was celebrating mass.

"You're such a clever thing, little sis. Do you know everything we have to say at mass?"

"Sure, most of it's here in this little book, and I've learned the rest by heart. When I grow up, I'm going to be a priest, Rosa."

"Marcela, women can't be priests. Only men can celebrate mass."

I deflated when I heard that. The cardboard cut in circles, the water, the wine…I'd spent hours cutting and pasting those bits of paper, hours. I knew I should say *The Lord is with you* and my imaginary parishioners should respond *And also with you*. I knew the mass off by heart.

"Why can't I be one?"

"Because that's what the Holy Church says, Marcela."

"But why?"

○●

Lord, there is no one like You. No one. No one. The chorus repeated the song's refrain without end. We arrived at the orphanage and distributed toys among the children who were tearing around our group. Rosa tried to keep everything under control but it was impossible. The toys were a powerful magnet for the orphans, who had turned into butterflies wheeling around. I put on my sheep costume as the priest said to me:

"Marcela, in the three years you've been with us you've proved yourself the best sheep we've ever had."

The priest was right about that. *No one can do what You do. No one. No one.* We sang along with the priest, applauding and jumping, sharing in the special delight that emanates from a toy in a child's hands.

"The Lord is with baaaaaa you baaaaaa," I shouted, shaking my sheep tail and waiting for a reply that never came. I tried something else. "We lift up baaaaa our hearts baaaaa." Nothing, no reply. But that was what was said at mass...

The priest stopped singing and came toward me, gesturing severely. He reprimanded me, told me off, said that you can't make fun of the sacred words of mass, that only a priest can say them, that you're a good little girl who makes a wonderful sheep but you can't say those things.

"So I can only say baaaaa?"

"Dressed as a sheep, yes."

"And if I dress up as a priest?"

"You can't, you stubborn child, mass is not a game."

It wasn't a game for me, either. Organizing others and making them do what you say is no game. I only wanted responses, to know the others were listening to me and would act in accordance with my words. The priest said one thing and everyone stood up, said another thing and they sat down; at another stage they even knelt. A whole group of people kneeling in front of the priest, depending on those words that would be repeated without end by other mouths, in other geographies, at other times. *We must respect what's sacred*, demanded the priest. *What's sacred is everywhere*, Rosa said in my defense.

○●

I couldn't understand what I was hearing. An accident. A bus. Crashing. A ravine. A thousand pieces. Rosa. I felt a pitiless mist descending on the world, smothering everything around me. My ears were blocked: I couldn't comprehend anything my father was telling me. My mother's arms hugged me tight. Screams. So much screaming. My legs wouldn't do what I wanted them to. No part of my body would. In my chest, I felt a black pit, a deep well where nothing could get in or out. Sheer emptiness. I looked over at the books Rosa had given me: Saint Augustine's *Confessions*, Kempis' *The Imitation of Christ,* and *Catechism of the Christian Doctrine.* In the distance, I felt my mother pulling me by the arm, as if I were a lifeless rubber doll. *Marcela, for the love of God, react, say something.* I looked at her, incredulous. *God? What are you talking about, mamá?* She worked herself half to death so others would know the word of God, but *for what, mamá? Tell me, for what? If God exists, he needs to give me back my sister right now!*

It's as if time has congealed in this white room. My recollections flicker across the wall opposite. What happened to my sister had a huge impact on me. It shook my world and all the religious beliefs I had; my faith fell away. Her death showed me the emptiness of those beliefs, though some ideas stayed with me and were useful with what came later. Religion is for slaves.

"Teacher, what news do you have for me today?" Romero has appeared out of nowhere, like always.

○●

You open the door, thinking it must be one of the insurgents knocking to ask for food. They're probably back from their morning patrol of the surrounding communities, where they recruit campesinos to their so-called armed struggle and get food supplies. The door opens and you see her. The bearing of a vicuña. She is white, so white. She looks like one of those statues of the Virgin María in the church. Where must she have come from. If the subversives see her in your house it will be so very bad for you, Modesta. She says she's from the capital. She wants to know what's happened in the hamlet, why the councilor isn't in the communal building. She asks a lot of questions. *I know nothing, mamacha, nothing at all.* The señorita doesn't understand that your calf is still hurting, that everything inside your head is hurting. *You should leave, señorita.*

She's stubborn, this woman from the coast, she doesn't understand. Won't understand. She's with a man. She seems like a good person but she's stubborn. *For your own good, mamacha, go away, get out of here.* They want you to tell them about yourself, if you've seen the subversives, if the military has come, to tell them, Modesta, to tell them. She fixes her gaze on you. Melanie, she says her name is. It must be Melanía, you must have heard wrong. She lifts up a device and you hear a click, and then another. Her gaze changes. The noise of bullets assaults your ears all of a sudden. Melanía and the man throw themselves to the floor. You warned them, Modesta, you warned them and they didn't listen. They didn't believe you. They didn't pay you any heed.

You see the terrorists running toward your house. You shut the door and hide away but it's useless. They kick the door down. A river of blood is flowing from the man's head. *Álvaro!* the señorita screams. They take her away. What are they going to do to you? You're shaking, Modesta; they've told you before that you're not to speak to anyone.

○●

She was a lump on the floor. It didn't matter what her name was, they were only interested in the two holes she had. Sheer emptiness to be filled up. No questions or need for replies. They knew all there was to know about this lump. But really, she meant nothing to them. Her four limbs were enough: with them she could be held down, immobilized, restrained. They wore rifles and the same clothes as the campesinos, with balaclavas or kerchiefs covering their faces. It was all the same, she was just a lump.

Blows to the face, abdomen; legs stretched out to infinity. *White traitor.* They line up to enjoy their part in the spectacle. No orifice is spared in this bloody dance. *Anticommunist journalist, we'll make an example of you for any others who come round here.* Only pain in this lump, like a tightened knot that could never come undone. How much longer could they keep it up? If only they'd stop now. Stop, stop, stop. *This is happening to you for being bourgeois, we'll force the ideology into you.* How long could they keep on doing it? *Go ahead, comrade.* How many more could there be? It hurts a lot. It's too much. There are too many of them. *Your story should have been about us, that way the genocidal State would see we're achieving a strategic balance.* Spurs tearing the fragile walls, which support and keep on supporting the procession despite the blood and excrement making their way between her legs.

○●

"It had to be long, but fruitful; it had to be bloody, but shining; it had to be grueling, but spirited and all-powerful. It has been said that the world is transformed by the barrel of a gun, and we're transforming it."

CENTRAL COMMITTEE, SHINING PATH

○●

I almost can't feel my body. I can hear voices but can't make out who they belong to. It's nighttime, or maybe this room doesn't have windows. A macabre dance begins amid the concert of rough voices. Hundreds of sharpened knives above hunks of gelatinous meat. The hunks of meat have been rotting for days, they stink terribly, and their greenish edges show marks where small, ravenous maggots have hatched. I can't remember how many days I've been here. Was it yesterday or has a week gone by? In the background, they're talking.

"When the high command finds out about your gross error they're going to stand you down, comrade."

"We're combatants, Comrade Marta, but we're also men."

"A combatant is disciplined; he doesn't let himself be guided by base impulses. There will be nothing to differentiate us from bourgeois reactionaries if we let these urges govern our actions."

"Like you don't know that our Leader has two women!"

"That's the Historic Standing Committee you're talking about; speak with respect. You will have to do a self-criticism at the next meeting, these urges are knocking the sense out of you."

"And as if you don't know that our comrade commissar of the rainforest region has his entourage of women."

The voices heat up. Someone comes running and desperately knocks at the door. Another searches for the dagger tucked into his boot. In the same instant that the dagger leaves its sheath and meets the cold of the night (is it night?), its owner gets a hail of machine-gun bullets to the middle of his chest. Someone else gets it to the forehead before he has the chance to feel pain or see how the earthen floor is irrigated with his brains. The other one, the woman, I think it's the one they called Comrade Marta, tries to hide. More gunfire. Soldiers are shooting at everything they can see in the room. Some of their feet almost slip in the pool of blood creeping across the floor. Metallic sounds. Smoke filling the bedroom. I scream, I'm not sure what I say, but I scream with the little strength I have left. Did my scream come out?

"Lieutenant, it's the photographer we're looking for!"

"Take her to the base, quick!"

"The rest are dead."

"Not that one; that terrorist is still alive!"

○●

She was a lump on the floor. It didn't matter what her name was, they were only interested in the two holes she had. Sheer emptiness to be filled up. The questions and answers would come later.

They would find out everything there was to know about this lump. But really, she meant nothing to them right now. Her four limbs were enough: with them she could be held down, immobilized, restrained. They wore black leather boots and khaki clothes, had nothing covering their faces. It was all the same, she was just a lump.

Blows to the face, abdomen; legs stretched out to infinity. *Fucking terrorist.* They line up to enjoy their part in the spectacle. No orifice is spared in this bloody dance. *Fucking subversive.* Only pain in this lump, like a tightened knot that could never come undone. How much longer could it go on? If only they'd stop now. Stop, stop, stop. *Your turn, soldier, finish the job, finish it off.* How long could they keep on doing it? *Give it to her hard, thrust all that ideology out of her.* How many more could there be? It hurts a lot. It's too much. There are too many of them. *Now you'll see how delicious it is when a sergeant gives it to you from behind, you'll never talk about your revolution again.* Spurs tearing the fragile walls, which support and keep on supporting the procession despite the blood and excrement making their way between her legs.

○●

"The incursion was a success, Lieutenant."

"Well then, we can tell the communities this is a liberated zone, cleansed of subversive elements. Now we need to find out how deep their ideology has penetrated, we need to know who was with the Shining Path and to treat those people as they deserve to be treated. And I want that terrorist to be singing the national anthem by the end of this. Understood, Sergeant?"

"Yes, Lieutenant."

"Is the photographer on her way to the capital?"

"Yes, Lieutenant, the navy helicopter arrived soon as we radioed them."

"If they'd reacted just as quick when these people asked for help, the story would have been different—these places are always forgotten. Sergeant, take care of getting my Uzi cleaned. Dismissed."

"Lieutenant, could I bother you with one more thing?"

"What's that?"

"The soldiers have been on the move and fighting for weeks, now. They deserve a little something to take their mind off things, wouldn't you say?"

"Sergeant, do what you will to keep your men happy, but I don't want to hear one word about it."

○●

She was a lump on the floor. It didn't matter what her name was, they were only interested in the two holes she had. Sheer emptiness to be filled up. They knew all there was to know about this lump. But really, she meant nothing to them. Her four limbs were enough: with them she could be held down, immobilized, restrained. They wore black leather boots and khaki clothes, balaclavas covering their faces. It was all the same, she was just a lump.

Blows to the face, abdomen; legs stretched out to infinity. *Fucking mountain whore.* They line up to enjoy their part in the spectacle. No orifice is spared in this bloody dance. *Lousy Indian.* Only pain in this lump, like a tightened knot that could never come undone. How much longer could it go on? If only they'd stop now. Stop, stop, stop. *Your turn, soldier, finish the job, finish it off.* How much longer could they keep it up? *Give it to her hard, these Indians can take anything.* How many more of them? It hurts a lot. It's too much. There are too many of them. *Now you'll see how delicious it is when a sergeant gives it to you from behind, you'll never feed those terrorists again.* Spurs tearing the fragile walls, which support and keep on supporting the procession despite the blood and excrement making their way between her legs.

○●

A plate of food; it is no trouble to dish up a plate of food, Modesta. You are always the one who nourishes, who provides. Whoever comes to your table will be welcomed, always, because you are the provider, tending to others, like the earth in which your generous broad beans, your silky-bearded corn, and your rock-shaped potatoes grow. Animals are made for sating man's hunger. The soldiers have asked for lunch, so you set about gathering together what's needed; you have to fix them something to eat. Another little hen that was poor Justina's. You cook it quick smart, otherwise you might be next. You cut into its neck with a blade. You'd like to do the same to the soldiers to put a stop to their abuse. You want to cry but squeeze your eyes shut and breathe deeply. You offer some coca leaves to the Apu and then stuff them into your mouth. You don't want to end up at the bottom of the ravine like half your community. You need to keep yourself alive because you're all little Abel has left. No matter who comes, they always kill us.

The coca leaf is bitter; you swallow the saliva and cry, your mouth numb. The hen has stopped kicking.

○●

More soldiers, and that music they always have playing in the background. My body reacted to almost nothing, had shut down to it all. They questioned me, wanted to wring out of me every last drop of information. How many of us there were, where we were. I wasn't about to tell those dogs anything. There was nothing they didn't do to my body. Anything could be a tool to inflict pain and humiliation. Water, electricity, cigarettes, wires, buckets, urine, their arms, hands, legs. All of it hurt, but my mind stayed strong and kept it together, unlike my limbs, which were almost dislocated from all the yanking. *This bitch is tough,* they murmured. *Hold her under again, see if that gets a reaction,* they said. *Now cut off the other nipple to make a pair,* they shouted at the soldier who was staring at my breasts. They were quick to cauterize any wounds so I wouldn't bleed to death, the cunning assholes.

I couldn't get used to the pain. It was simply there, like hunger or thirst could simply be there. Something else to break me. Always there. Hit, interrogated, cut, bruised, broken, bitten, rammed, lacerated, stabbed, muddied, kicked, humiliated, dirtied, divided, tied up, dunked, suffocated, choked. I was confident of our triumph despite my body's shrieks of defeat. *Sometimes I go to the capital to get orders from the Central Committee.* My body talked; it wasn't me. They told the officer.

They would prep me for transportation to a jail in the capital. They would not break me, they would not break me, they will not break me...

○●

A mouthful of air. And another. And another. But it doesn't stop, Modesta, it doesn't stop. You put up with the breathing, but it's uncontrollable. It starts spreading through your whole body. It goes from your chest to your arms. They shout. In the distance, they shout. It's about to start again. There it is. Taking over your whole body. All of it. Fear. Pure fear in your veins. It buries into your soft tissue and holes up there. What's this? Electricity? Dizziness overcomes you, you're about to fall but you don't. You know you have a seed inside you that you don't want. What's going to come out of you? Your head spins round and round but you don't fall. Your chest hurts, your chest caves in and your lungs stick to your back. They get tangled in your ribs. You're going mad. The faces were always the same, the same eyes, the same voices, the same hands, the same cocks. All the same. Everything hurt in the same way. Get off, get off me, the only thing you could say while they savaged you, ripping into your middle as they had done to so many other women in this very hamlet, in hundreds of hamlets. You always screamed, but knew in advance it was useless. Made a battlefield, your body has become acutely vulnerable. You're still you. Your nails, your hair, your teeth chatter. Your legs tremble, you want to run but can't leave. The food. Quick, the food, they say. Dive into that pot and disappear. Boil yourself up with those chickens.

Let your flesh turn white white white. It's already white. Deathly white. Your hand shakes. Your arms shake. The pot shakes. Fear. The floor shakes. How many more times? How many more days? What's going to come out of you? If only someone would steady you, hug you, take care of you. You press your mouth shut but your teeth won't stop. They won't stop won't stop won't stop. You're going to die. You don't want to die. You'll die. It would be preferable to die. Breathe. Live. Breathe. Tremble. Live.

○●

I don't want to move. I can't move. Everything hurts. I wish they would leave me like this, still, motionless. In a static shot. I want to shut myself in a capsule, in the fetal position. My body is open and exposed. I can't leave this bedroom. Outside, even the breeze might knock me down. All the world around me as if it wants to push its way inside me. I watch it from afar. In the distance. A capsule, a shield, a shell. Far off. The world can and will keep on without me. I'm here and I'm me, but the world goes on. Parties, people, clubs, soldiers, newspapers. No one hears a thing. They don't see it, either. It's as if I'm not here, but everything goes on and on and on. The world doesn't spin, just keeps on. Who even cares where it's off to. Everything hurts. I don't want even the sheet to graze me, or the quilt. Nothing. Any graze is a threatening sword. I press my legs together. I'm an open wound. Close up, body. Close up, before the world gets in. Close up.

○●

the bonds strengthen like this bloody womb everyone together we're all one inside her she who won't look at us now or talk now soaked bloody chest the women everyone brothers everyone the entire troop in her in them in the whores the indians the terrorists the journalists the daughters the mothers all of them it grows more until what point it looks like it's not enough it grows it hardens on everyone everyone huge and hard present your identity card open her divide her slice her penetrate her cut her everyone brothers just a hole that's what they're for rip into it break it your turn you and you and him and him and them everyone brothers ranks comrade soldier combatant drive into her sergeant revolution army committee navy it grows more a bit of fun it grows more we multiply in the pampa the mountains huge like the hills we burst in river emptied joint forces we divide the mountain we fracture the dawn we penetrate the land we slash the sky we open everything up nothing is closed to us we're brothers

○●

"The experience of all liberation movements has shown that the success of a revolution depends on how much the women take part in it."

LENIN

79

○●

Here they are again, Modesta. They're approaching, you know how their steps sound when they're hungry not for your food but for you. For you, Modesta, for you. You know the beat of boots, rhythm of a cicada thrum, are a bad sign. But this time you don't manage to get little Abel out of the house. There isn't the time. Your son, there in the room, Modesta. Abel scoots under his bed, quick as a guinea pig. They don't give a damn about your pleas. *Just lie down, you know how this goes. Just calm down.* They're on top of you already, Modesta. You pray before your son's eyes, Modesta. Your son's eyes. Two eyes, five soldiers. It's nighttime, you think, maybe Abel can't see anything and the light from those two candles doesn't reach his eyes and your body. Five soldiers, they don't even shout anymore, don't sling insults, they act as if it's a transaction. So many times. You don't scream anymore. What for. As if they were taking a dump. Abel's eyes. You see a gleam. You turn your face. Soldier sweat. There's your son, looking your way. He's looking at you. Does he see you? What does he see? Is his mother what he sees? An onslaught inside you and you smile, Modesta. Your son's eyes. You smile. Five soldiers, but you smile. Your body split in two. You smile for Abel's eyes. You clean yourself off, Modesta. Your son's eyes. Do you feel anything, Modesta? *What are you looking at, Indian?* You turn your head. *You were looking at something, damn it, what the fuck were you looking at?* The soldier turns and sees him there. Abel. His eyes. One soldier stays inside you, the others pull Abel from beneath the bed. You didn't want to look, but you saw it when your son stopped seeing, when they turned out his light forever. Abel, his light gone. Never again.

His eyes bulged out like balloons. They zip up their flies and take Abel to the health post at the base. *A child shouldn't see these things*, the soldier who is still inside you says. *He might grow into a pervert*, he adds emphatically, thrusting one more time and spilling all over your insides.

○●

You think about death with a regularity that astonishes and disgusts you. At the same time, you hate it as much as you could hate anything, though you know death is not just any old thing. The thing to remember is it's just that: a thing, an object, something material. Who knows, maybe you could try selling it to someone. Get some benefit out of it. Who would want to buy it from you? No one would pay for your death. But even if it's worth just a few coins, it's truly yours, your death, truly yours. The only thing that really belongs to you.

○●

dah dit dah dit behind dah he snaps his fingers liquor in his blood everyone in the capital dah dit dah dit he dances with three of them now it's down to two he dances with her applause she straightens her hair dum dum dum Do you remember how it went? she raises her arms dum dum dum crosses her legs dah dit dit dit spins spins spins everyone else applauds smiles sings they think we're in the mountains let's dance dum dum dum spin again spin again dum dum move your feet they look at each other smile

he she three now two all the women want to dance with the
leader they dance circle of comrades mao lenin marx watch us
from their position on the wall dah dit dit dit give it your all comrades applause now everyone hold hands dah dit dum dum holding
on out in foot forward foot back to the side moving forward in
a circle dum leadership dum leader and another comrade singing
applause applause applause dum dum dum jump jump jump everyone in a circle look at the camera dum dum in hiding jubilant

○●

Don't they watch the news? They own newspapers, news bulletins,
magazines, but they don't see it. Don't they know what's happening? They're killing people, so many people, so much blood.
Pain. Revulsion. Blood. Rage. It's an avalanche about to surge
into our faces, on our doorsteps. *Did you hear about Ana María's
brother-in-law, the army general?* The news spreads. *They killed him
on his way home from the ministry. It looks as if they followed him
and then peppered his car with bullets.* The avalanche has arrived.
What is there to understand when nothing is as it seems, when
the words for things go missing and get replaced with others that
don't fit? *They're even killing generals, just imagine what could happen
to the rest of us.* Things that don't make sense. The music gulps
down the questions and hacks them up, transformed into cigarette
smoke. Skin and breath. Faces and bodies. *The photos were in all
the newspapers, the poor man, they destroyed him.* Ana María avoids
talking about it, has thrown this party to take her mind off it.
No one asks her anything directly. They don't approach her, either.

I decide to breach the distance and give her a hug. Surprised, she stays there a moment, not letting go of me. Then she smiles with some difficulty. *Mel, tell me everything you saw in the mountains.* How do I tell her? I don't even know how many of them there were. I was a rag, darling, a rag. There was a woman among them. I saw her. But I lie. I did count them. Later I cursed myself for having done so. One, two, three, four and they kept on. They kept going, kept going, five, five, five, six, how many, I was a wound, a rag, four, two, three, one, five, five, five. Useless to keep on counting. My body still doesn't want to count.

○●

The sun. So much sun on this summer's day. I stretch out on the sand and there's nothing for it but to remember, as soon as the heat seeps between my legs and the sea breeze laps freely at my skin. If the breeze keeps up its lapping it will create a snaking electrical current. That electricity that starts in my middle, like when I was in kindergarten. I was three, maybe four. The teacher told us to cut paper into geometric shapes to paste on a piece of cardboard. When the pots of paste were opened, the party started. I loved the smell of the white paste and sank my nose into the thick and sticky milk. I sank into that milk, never my mother's milk. She was no longer around and her face had gone from my memory. Fed up with cutting and sticking the pieces of paper, I dropped the scissors and stood up. I pressed my pelvis against the table, rubbing myself, anxious, faster and faster. I balanced on that surface and the delicious, shooting vertigo opened a path.

A maelstrom in my middle. I didn't have a name for it, I just let myself be swept away by that electricity, which grew stronger and burst from my center through the rest of my body. My arms bent with the effort of supporting my weight and maintaining that strategic balance. I would have kept on like that for hours if the teacher hadn't pulled me away from the table and out of the classroom. Unplugged from pleasure. I was drenched in sweat and, without her needing to say one word, I took myself off to the detention room. Now, remembering and imagining that picture—the girl rubbing herself against the table like an ardent pigeon—I can't help but laugh. Might I have taught my fellow classmates and my teacher something? It's incredible how relaxed and free we are when we're still innocent. For the few minutes it lasted, I delighted in the sensation that I still didn't have a name for. No fear of anything, not the least bit of censorship. No one else existed. On that cold table, in the middle of my pleasure, I was the center of the universe.

I rise back to the surface. Violence has birthed me again. Speak, body. Cry out, body.

○●

When I developed the pictures, it was as if everything had taken on a different dimension. In some it seemed like the photographic fixer had favored a definition of certain bodies over others. Few faces were possible to distinguish, but there was one in particular that stood out. It was a girl, very young, standing there, her gaze focused on nothing. Around her, several bodies, out of focus.

Some people are running, also out of focus. The sharpness of her image draws attention to her expression: it's not incredulous, not angry, not distant, not accepting, not in pain. She has seen something like this before. It's as if she is beyond the massacred bodies, has arrived at an understanding that escapes the rest of us. The sense of having gone beyond some limit. I'd like to ask her: What did you come to know? Why did all this happen?

Another group of photographs seemed cut off, as if the images demanded to escape the frame   prolonging the gazes of the men, women, and children contained within those four drawn borders. There's the one of the town hazy with smoke. The smell I'll never be free of. These are photos that push you to look outside the frame, that gesture at all that hasn't been captured. How much is outside the frame? What stories will get away?

○●

Community member Carlos Quechán has accused your husband of being a terrorist informant, a sergeant notifies you. You try to explain the resentment and fury Carlos harbored toward your husband. They're outright lies. How could they believe him? Where could you go look for your Gaitán? Wherever your husband has got to by now, there's nothing you can do. Just forget him. Nothing, Modesta, nothing. You won't see him again.

You pick up off the floor the pieces of you that are left over. Sometimes you're in your right mind, sometimes you feel empty. You forget what you think; you wish you'd go mad. Your head hurts a lot, your body hurts. You haven't felt right since that day in the communal room, when they killed Justina and the others, when the whole world got turned the wrong way up. Pachacuti. Earthquake. World standing on its head. It's not what it used to be, now everything's something else.

A little girl came out of you. Who knows which seed she sprouted from. You fill a bowl with broth from the day's sacrificed chicken. The noodles look like bullets floating in the green plastic bowl. Water with white noodles. After the first sip, a river of tears flows from your eyes, uncontrollable, as if they've turned into waterfalls. The tears don't stop. You feel as if in that river all the pain of your body is flowing out. And you want to talk.

"I'm fed up. I'm worn out."

Gaitán, I miss you. I look at your photo and miss you more. Among the lines of my hands, you appear. Finally. You cross my life line and divide it. Here you are, in this hollow of skin and sweat that yearns for you. This is your new home: the palm of my memories. I feel my body trembling again. That wave of fear is coming over me once more. The floor starts to tremble. Breathe in, breathe out. It presses at my chest and starts to make its way toward my arms and stomach. It is fear. Or, worse yet, its sire, the fear of fear. I look toward the Apu, from where my parents must be watching me, from afar; they died before all this started. I bring my hands under control—they're cold and don't want to move—and, just like they did to Justina, with one slash I cut fear's throat. I let it bleed dry so it will leave my body. I escape.

○●

I set out, without my little Abel. They couldn't stem the bleeding. Life left his eyes. I mostly walk at nighttime, listening for the puma. May it not gobble me up. I don't stop until I get to another hamlet, where I ask the women, *Water, mamachas, water, food.* Food means a few tiny potatoes swimming in a broth of water and salt. *That's all we have. The soldiers set fire to the grains so we wouldn't have anything to eat.* But those shameless men haven't left yet. They knock on the door again. I know the sound of those hungry boots. *Mamacha, let me answer it, I know them.* When they open the door it's just one soldier, all by himself, saying he wants food. *Grab him, mamachas.* They take a while to hold him down. He rears up. *You scoundrel.* I grab the pot of boiling soup and pour it over his parts. He screams as if his soul is escaping him. His rifle has fallen down, and we lift it to strike him across the head. *So you're not so brave after all, little soldier. You're not going to do any of that rotten business to anyone else, you swine.* He has fainted. We leave him lying there. *Let's leave, mamachas, let's get out of here.* They follow me; we'll continue on together. I hold tight to the rifle.

○●

I don't know what's in store for me tomorrow. How can I think about the future? The future is no more than a word, and now I have to worry about what my companions and I will eat, what we'll feed my daughter and their children. They'd better not mess with us again, we're not fields for the taking: they can't come plant their seed whenever the urge strikes. *I don't know how you do it, Modesta, but I don't love my little one. He came out of me, but I don't love him. It's hard for me to watch him there, the poor little thing, defenseless, if I don't take care of him he'll die, but here I am, looking after him by force of habit, nothing more, sometimes I think it would be best if he died, if he just died, it makes me angry... What will happen when he grows up and asks about his father?* She started to cry. The thought of abandoning her child reminded her of being abandoned by the Apus. And when he says to me, *Mamá, don't I have a father?*

Her baby took a few short steps toward the door. He looked at us and stuffed a hand in his mouth. He squatted and started scratching the floor, then ate a bit of dirt. My friend and I let him do it. *I don't love him, Modesta.* And he kept eating dirt while neither of us made a move to stop him. Is my Abel an angel already? And little Enrique? Are they in heaven?

I wasn't about to tell anyone how one day I went to leave my baby by the river. How could I live with that baby? I also wanted to leave her. It was possible someone might find her and give her a good life. But there was almost no one around these parts anymore. She might die and everything would end right there for her. Either case was better than having her with me. I dropped the basket and ran back to the hamlet. Not even ten minutes went by of all that running around, my heart about to jump out of me, when I decided to go back. Breathing deeply, I walked toward the river. The basket was still there. A young vicuña was lapping at the water nearby. It stopped drinking when it sensed my presence. It moved toward the basket and sniffed it a little.

The baby had been so quiet, but now she started, out of nowhere, to bawl. She cried so loud. I took her with me. What was I going to do? She was so tiny. What would her life be without me, barely a pampa devoid of animals, a sad river, or a bald hill. She came out of me.

○●

If we don't bring it all under control, there's no way of establishing order, he thinks. The same room, he's the third since all this started. But there is not just one, now there are two who think, organize, give orders. They're everywhere. The two of them are seated face to face; no one occupies the head of the table. They talk, look at each other; one's slight movement of the eyebrows is read by the other. *It has to be very carefully located, a well-aimed blow.* The other scrawls a few things but doesn't lower his gaze. The pen moves mechanically. Notes that will later become a decree, or not. The color of their suits is the same grayish. *We'll tell the general and he'll take care of it.* One of them wavers, the one who has the official title. And if they're not? he voices his misgivings. And if they are? replies the other. *They also do such things, no matter the losses.* He's worried they might be civilians; moreover, it's the capital, it won't slip under the radar, it will be in all the papers and we already know what the human rights people are like. Isn't there more information from Intelligence? He tells him this is the surest piece of information they have. He wants to know more about the leaders. *We have to take down the leadership right away.* They know there has been progress in that regard.

At any moment the leaders will be captured. They will wait for new developments. *But we have to be forceful about this.* They're civilians who will be having a good time. A party. It won't cross anyone's mind. They won't even be able to react. The two of them adjust their glasses at the same time. He clears his throat, a little uncomfortable. He owes the other a lot. Why wait? *We'll give the order to the general that they should go all out.*

○●

While I wait for the major, I overhear the soldiers whispering. *That terrorist looks a bit butch.* They laugh. I turn to glare right into their mindless sheep eyes and they stiffen, pretend they don't see me. Miserable fools. What do they know about women? They probably call me butch because of my short hair. They don't know the feminine is the origin of everything. It's ferment, magma, purification, creation. The dawn that will rise when the revolution is complete. Teresa of Ávila knew what it was to be a woman. She had so many daughters, she lived on many more times over than if she had married. Why have a husband when you can create more without one? Reproduce an ideal, strength, a revolution. That's where I went wrong; I have to think it over, examine it, perform a self-criticism. Why did we take so long? When should I have kept shooting? When should I not have shot?

○●

To become military commissar of the central zone I had to go through so much first. The appointment was a gift from Fernanda. There were more than enough men. Fernanda knew that. They had known Comrade Felipe longer than they'd known me. Felipe thought he would be made commissar.

Our Leader had identified the need for death squads to ensure the success of the revolution. My chances of joining the leadership were not all that high, the male majority preferred Comrade Felipe for sure. He longed to destroy, to be on the frontline. Felipe believed blindly in the armed struggle. Fernanda made it clear that all military commissars had a central ideological mission: to remember, always, that the party rules, not the barrel of the gun. I saw Felipe clench his fist and fix his gaze on Fernanda. If he could have, he'd probably have shoved a stick of dynamite into her gut. *Pure ideology is a fallacy, comrades, without the barrel of the gun there is no power.* He said it all by himself, and all by himself he slipped the noose around his own neck. The Leader intervened and with one slash cut off the stupidity *The party rules over the barrel of the gun; thought dominates, not force.* His words quashed Felipe's aspirations. Fernanda had set the trap and the brute had walked right into it. Silence was my strength. The path had been cleared.

"It still surprises me to know that, with so many men available for the position, they ended up choosing you, teacher."

"You think I wasn't capable?"

My sharp retort takes Romero by surprise, which he attempts to hide by averting his gaze.

"Not at all, teacher, you're more than capable. What I mean is that the natural choice would have been Comrade Felipe."

The natural choice. You're just like everyone else, Major. Whatever you think, it's all the same to me. What worries me is why you're going to such pains to get along with me. I hate those snakes who think they're capable of manipulating a woman but don't know how to proceed with their objective. I, in contrast, knew how to proceed. Fernanda had paved the way for me. I made the most of it and asked for the floor. Each of us had to be willing to pay the price. To give one's life for the revolution is the most sacred honor for any combatant. That's how I sealed my position in the party. Words, Major Romero, words, in the right moment, in the right ear. They chose me.

○●

pachacuti between the buildings pachacuti in the capital bomb cars fire the vehicle was meant for the bank but it hit the building bomb drizzle of blood as far as the park the roads the municipality the schools the sea the doctors' offices the workplaces the ministries revolution boom it wearied of the countryside bleeding ear glass glass city ravine bomb the street seller screams everyone runs bomb bomb bomb blood as well *bastards* her leg is gone his son among the rubble lost arm shattered bones bomb spattered walls cracked columns police officers firefighters broken windows a hand falls bomb fingers bomb fingers bomb hands bomb fire *bastards* burnt face everyone screams can scream bomb bleeding wounds she falls down *bastards* elsewhere they dance in hiding bomb they run what was up is now down rise up bomb pachacuti you heard bomb tarata

○●

"Lord, why do you send so much death our way?
Why do you look on as we kill one another?"

ANDEAN SONG

○●

And if I tell you about it? Tell you every last bit, Daniela? Something lodged in my body but it's not there anymore. Why did I come to Paris? To get it out, a fruit that shouldn't exist, that holed up in my body against my will. I came because I wanted to see you. The city of drizzle was hemming me in. You cause a river in my mouth. The center of the universe on the tip of your tongue. My body screams five five five, but that scream no longer resounds. Now five means your fingers, which travel across my skin. Surrendering to the desire in your eyes, the scream becomes a moan. This is what makes living worth it. You become a river in my mouth. Lake, sea, ocean in me. Now you navigate. You drink the water I give you. Our legs are intertwined, they moor you to me, a liquid knot. The chords of your pleasure constrict my waist. Your fingernails nest in my back, another victory. This is why, Daniela, this is what it was for. You loosen the knot and open a space between my legs. Your fingers are serpents that guide me in their dance. A welcome invasion.

○●

"Ready to go hunting?"

Jimena is thrilled to see me after all this time between the mountains and Paris. Willing to follow me on my forays to the club, always just a phone call away. That hasn't changed.

"I've been away so long, I'm out of practice."

"Out of practice? You? As if, Mel, your aim's always right on. Whoever you look at falls hard, and today's Friday."

Jimena lights up a Marlboro. We're in my SUV on our way to Kraken. The band Frágil is on the radio: *Hunters stalking here and there flushing out their prey in the city, roaring motors everywhere.* The drizzle dampens the roads. Now I just need to forget the campesina who, in her confusion, called me Melanía. Forget Álvaro. It was a game of Russian roulette in the mountains and the bullet happened to get him. What I happened to get was something different. Poor Álvaro. I want to kill a man. Kill five, to be honest. Watch them suffer, bleeding out.

When I look at Jimena, so cheerful and vibrant, learning to smile again comes easy. We're off hunting, to see who will get lucky tonight. A few dogs appear nearby. They sicken me, I don't want to look at them anymore. I accelerate; the green lights along the avenue usher us through in a wave that doesn't stop. Open. The city of drizzle opens up before me and I dissolve into her. Everything can go back to normal. Everything will be normal again, or almost everything. *They step out into the night, they set the tone, they hop into their ride. They're ready for anything.*

The drizzle hits the windshield. Tonight the air is fine and fresh, light, so different from that thick air in the mountains.

As if the dead bodies had become particles of air and wanted to come back to life in our nasal passages. As if they were saying *We're still here.* I think about Paris and Daniela. Jimena lights another cigarette and offers me one. Perfect for overpowering my sense of smell. *There are some who fail, others who never try. That's when they decide, the river has run dry.* My hand demands the camera. I'll have to go back into that hell.

○●

I have the rest of my life to think and keep on remembering. All the time in the world to think about my daughter, too. How is she? How much has she grown? Does she remember me? The dawn has left her without her mamá. Will she understand? Will she forgive me? Now's the time to weigh up each detail, each excess, because we made no mistakes. There were none. Violence is the midwife of history. There were excesses that should have been contained. Perfection is found in containment. Through asceticism, one can achieve anything. That's why I think and go over everything; I have the rest of my life to do so.

"We're going to take you to see your leader, teacher. He's going to sign the agreement set out by the government. Peace has come to us at last," Major Romero announces. "Come on, why so serious, I know this is exciting news for you. It's okay to get swept up in it."

"Control is the line separating actions that meet with success from those that do not."

"You always think so much, teacher. Look, so you can get ready to meet him, we found a few things your leader wrote.

This one's priceless: 'Whatever remains will be burned and its ashes will scatter to the four corners of the earth so that not even sinister memories of what must never return are left behind, because it cannot and must not ever return.' It must not ever return: he himself said it."

"You must have made that up. Something that never departed can't 'return': exploitative governments, treacherous politicians, abused campesinos, exploited workers. We won't be here, and it won't happen in our name, but the onward march of history continues and it can only be birthed with violence."

Romero keeps looking at me and shuffles his papers. In his eyes I see that other man I can never forget. A coup de grâce would suit Romero nicely. I notice an odd-looking insect making its way across the white melamine, closing in on his documents. I exterminate it with one slap and roughly wipe my hand on the table.

○●

The Apus remembered us at last. A good number of us women have decided to work together, to try to get back something, even just a tiny bit, of the lives we led before. We weave. The rifle is hidden away. Some women are quiet; others, more talkative.

My little one regards me with her big eyes. I don't want to remember because all that hurts a lot. It still hurts. Memory is a sword in my heart stirring it all up. But there's my little girl, so tiny, a little guinea pig. Mine and who else's, I wonder. There were so many of them. She has five little fingers on each hand

and five little toes on each foot. She is whole, perfect. It took all my courage to take her to the civil registry. She was so tiny and fragile, with her huge eyes, black and bright, which confronted me with my own reflection of rage. I might learn to love her one day. The señor at the registry took down her details with those letters that look like mountains, a cup handle, bent irons. The only thing I thought to say when he asked about the little one's father was *Soldier.*

It's been almost two years since I got away. I've thought about death a lot. When I remember the sasachakuy time my heart hurts. Difficult years, they were. Each time I remember, it hurts. Each time I forget, life seems peaceful. Sometimes we stop our work and another woman comes to join us. One takes up some thread and starts weaving. The threads cross over each other and the fabric grows. The weavers saying things. *Just between us—we're all women.* That's the only reason I talk. Another thread. Our voices weaving.

○●

My heart felt like it was tightening and there was pressure on my chest snap the length of yarn grows snap they remember snap *I hate sloppy seconds* her husband said splat memories snap like a machete blow snap snap it sounds snap mouth snap bruised snap no teeth crack rotting inside snap *I reported it but they paid me no heed* rip rip rip the fabric rips flesh snap they cry break them split them his sister his daughter his mother his wife snap his grandmother kerosene his *now we're all miserable with no family* stab her in the gut snap boots balaclavas uzi fal bullet bullet bullet

ten twenty thirty crack entire battalion comes in bomb crack no
one hears soldiers sadism comrades a little fun terrorists crack
she was already dead and they kept going going going another thread
brains in the corners kerosene burns guts fire splat fire snap fire
quick walk for fuck's sake stab him crack *señora help us move the
bodies* she opens her mouth doesn't scream nothing comes out
she can't she shrieks unfolding dawn unfolding brains unfolding
revolution attacked splat a piece splat open flesh crack thread *the
body was found by his other daughter* splat kick crack her son her
father her brother her husband crack her grandfather snap the
pack feeds on your face your eyes your tongue they devour pieces
raw kerosene she remembers snap *if you don't eat we'll slaughter
you* stab pampa hungry grave snap they don't exist body smoke
body lump dread dread thread so much his neck dread arm fingers
teeth dread breasts dread nipples thread blood in the streets dread
machete ax pincushion crack silence weave scream weave pain
crack *pregnant with pain* snap snap dagger shut up bullet shut up
bullet annihilate *you must also have sisters you must also be born of
woman* snap remember we live much thread we live we cry out
another thread we live many voices so many too many all of it.

THE AUTHOR WOULD LIKE TO THANK:

Diamela Eltit and Antonio Muñoz Molina, for their reading, advice and generosity.

My colleagues and friends from the literary workshops led by Diamela Eltit in NYU, especially Margarita Almada, Lorea Canales, Carolina Gallegos-Anda, Sandra García, Mar Gómez, Javier Guerrero, Felipe Hernández, Madeline Millán, Elisa Montesinos, Alejandro Moreno, Jorge Ninapayta, Joanne Rodríguez and Rubén Sánchez.

Margarita Saona, Julio Villanueva Chang, Martín Pinedo, Leonardo Dolores and everyone at Animal de invierno, for their time and dedication.

My parents, always.

Ana Ribeiro, for the long road traveled. Words aren't enough to describe how much this novel and I owe you.

In an article in *El País*, Spanish writer Antonio Muñoz Molina noted contemporary Peruvian novelists' aptitude for creating narratives infused with historical and political reality: novels that set out to capture the real. *Blood of the Dawn*'s allusions to events of the recent past—some oblique, others named, but all with real-world equivalents unmistakable for Peruvian readers—make it not out of place, I don't think, to name those events here so readers of the translation are better equipped to find out more.

There is another reason to do so. Historian Cecilia Méndez G. has argued that, while the Shining Path insurrection has had an indelible effect on Peruvian society, it is a period that many Peruvians, especially those who live in the capital, do their utmost to forget. Dwelling on this "time of fear,"—or, for Quechua speakers, the "sasachakuy [difficult] time."—which claimed at least 70,000 lives, is too painful. The urgency of representation present in *Blood of the Dawn* is a courageous response to this amnesia, a demand to remember as much as an attempt to represent, a pointing toward the real as well as a transformation of that real by means of the imagination.

So, a list: the 1983 Lucanamarca massacre, the 1985 Accomarca massacre, the 1986 prison riots and massacres (including at the women's prison in Santa Mónica), the 1991 Barrios Altos massacre and the 1992 Tarata bombing. Reference is also made to a 1989 video that features the Shining Path leader dancing to "Zorba the Greek" with the high command.

The Quechua words I decided not to gloss mostly represent complex ideas from the Andean cosmovision, where features of the landscape are invested with spirit. Some rough approximations: Apus are sacred mountains or powerful mountain spirits; Pachamama is something like Mother Earth; and Pachacuti is a space-time turnover, a chaotic time where everything is turned on its head after a thousand-year cycle of the earth ends and the next begins. Another Quechua term derives from Andean experiences of colonialism: the Pishtaco is a mythological bogeyman, often a white stranger, who kills Andean individuals to steal their body fat. Body fat is a sign of vitality and beauty in the Andes. Add to this the Andeans' horror on observing the way Spanish conquistadores treated their wounds with the fat of their enemies' corpses and you have the makings of a myth set to endure. Its modern incarnations include the belief that sugar-mill machinery uses human fat as grease—a critique of Western capitalism if ever there were one.

Blood of the Dawn manages to compress a great deal into very little space, which has made translating it an absorbing and sometimes daunting challenge. One remarkable feature is the way a single idea is expressed twofold through content and form. For example, the plot's focus on women as drivers of history is reflected in how their stories are told: Salazar Jiménez reminds us that language is a means of articulating systems of domination, patriarchy among them, through her steadfast refusal to use the full sentences dictated by standard grammar. In another example, *Blood of the Dawn* wrestles with how we might begin to represent violence in light of the physical and psychic damage it wreaks. The fragmentary nature of the narrative—its rapid switching among scenes, perspectives, grammatical tenses and persons, and especially the sections that turn away from grammatical organization almost completely—articulates the near impossibility of relating trauma while at the same time offering up an ambitious attempt to do the same.

A key challenge in bringing across all this compressed complexity was trying to reflect the different voices of the protagonists. These voices are painted with Quechua-inflected Spanish (in sentence structure as much as vocabulary), Maoist ideology, echoes of Catholic catechism, the language of elitist prejudice and racism, and much more besides. Through the rhythm of Modesta's voice, I hope I have conveyed something of the repetitions that call to mind predominantly oral cultures, where lodgment in the listener's memory is often favored over economy of expression. With Marcela/Marta, I have tried to emphasize the sense of indoctrination into Shining Path ideology. For example, when the word "*encarnado*" ("in the flesh," "embodied," "personified") is used to describe the way she exemplifies the revolution, I opted to include a biblical allusion by translating "*revolución encarnada*" as "the revolution made flesh" in an echo of both the 1611 and standard versions of the King James Bible, "the Word was made flesh" (John 1:14). Attentive readers will notice other biblical echoes throughout. And as for Melanie, where possible I included cultural references that would suit her milieu, such as when she describes the movements of a café as being like a dance. After a café-wide pause, she describes this dance as starting up again with the verb "*reiniciar*." Given the dance-related metaphors of the passage and the high cultural capital of her milieu, why not use, instead of my initial thought ("resume"), the word "reprise," which also means a repeated passage in music? In the case of the lyrics scattered through Melanie's sections, in my translations I have privileged rhyme over, in some cases, the exact meaning. I have done this so that they are more likely to be understood as lyrics, while at the same time I have tried to ensure that the thematic echoes of the lyrics remain intact.

The translation has benefitted from the input of many people. Thank you to Percy Cáceres Manrique for mentioning a book he'd seen on a flyer stuck to a telegraph pole in Arequipa, which he thought sounded like something I'd like to read; to the wonderful people of Herhúsið, Siglufjörður, Iceland, where I did most of the first draft of the translation; and to Jarrah Strunin and Paul Begovich for their astute suggestions. And my deepest thanks go to Claudia, for her enthusiasm, faith, generosity, and encouragement.

A NOTE ON QUOTATIONS

The epigraph on p. 3 is Clayton Eshleman and José Rubia Barcia's translation of César Vallejo's poem "Los nueve monstruos"—"The Nine Monsters"—in *César Vallejo: The Complete Posthumous Poetry*, Berkeley and LA: University of California Press, 1978, p. 173.

The quoted lines of poetry on p. 64 are also Clayton Eshleman and José Rubia Barcia's translation of César Vallejo, this time of his "There is a man mutilated...", which can be found on p. 29 of the abovementioned book.

On p. 55, both the "Dicotyledonous group" and "Let's see. Don't let it transcend..." poetry lines are Clayton Eshleman's translation of César Vallejo's "V.", in *The Complete Poetry: A Bilingual Edition*, Berkeley and LA: University of California Press, 2007.

The Marx, Lenin, Mao Tse Tung, Engels and Lenin quotes, used on pp. 5, 19, 36, 46, and 80 respectively, as well as the oath taken by Shining Path members on p. 46, are drawn from popular sources.

The quote from the Shining Path Central Committee on p. 71 is my translation.

The Andean song lyrics on p. 93 and song lyrics based on Jeremiah 10:6 on p. 67 are my translations.

The song lyrics on p. 28 are from Charly García's "Demoliendo hoteles" from his 1984 album *Piano Bar*, and are my translation.

The song lyrics on p. 44 are from Miguel Bose's "Amante bandido" from his 1984 album *Bandido*, and are my translation.

The song lyrics on p. 94–95 are from Frágil's "Avenida Larco" from their 1980 album *Avenida Larco*, and are my translation.

CLAUDIA SALAZAR JIMÉNEZ, born in Lima, Peru in 1976, one of the most recognized Peruvian writers of her generation, is also a literary critic, professor, cultural manager, and the founder of the literary journal Fuegos de Arena. She studied literature at the Universidad Nacional Mayor de San Marcos and holds a PhD from NYU. She edited the anthologies "Escribir en Nueva York" (2014) about Hispanic American Narrators and "Voces para Lilith" (2011) on contemporary South American women writers, and is also the founder and director of PERUFEST, the first Peruvian cinema festival in New York. Her debut novel *Blood of the Dawn* was awarded the Las Americas Narrative Prize of Novel in 2014. She also received the TUMI-USA Award in 2015. Her most recent publication is the collection of short stories *Coordenadas Temporales* (2016). She is currently based in New York City.

ELIZABETH BRYER is a translator and writer from Australia. Her translations have previously appeared in *Words without Borders* and *Overland Literary Journal*, and her writing about translation has been published in *Sydney Review of Books*. In 2016 she curated an edition of *Seizure Online*, which she dedicated to translated fiction and poetry. Her creative writing has been widely anthologized in publications including *The Lifted Brow*, *Meanjin* and *Best Australian Science Writing*.

Thank you all
for your support.
We do this for you,
and could not do
it without you.

DEAR READERS,

Deep Vellum Publishing is a 501c3 nonprofit literary arts organization founded in 2013 with a threefold mission: to publish international literature in English translation; to foster the art and craft of translation; and to build a more vibrant book culture in Dallas and beyond. We are dedicated to broadening cultural connections across the English-reading world by connecting readers, in new and creative ways, with the work of international authors. We strive for diversity in publishing authors from various languages, viewpoints, genders, sexual orientations, countries, continents, and literary styles, whose works provide lasting cultural value and build bridges with foreign cultures while expanding our understanding of how the world thinks, feels, and experiences the human condition.

Operating as a nonprofit means that we rely on the generosity of tax-deductible donations from individual donors, cultural organizations, government institutions, and foundations. Your donations provide the basis of our operational budget as we seek out and publish exciting literary works from around the globe and build a vibrant and active literary arts community both locally and within the global society. Deep Vellum offers multiple donor levels, including LIGA DE ORO ($5,000+) and LIGA DEL SIGLO ($1,000+). Donors at various levels receive personalized benefits for their donations, including books and Deep Vellum merchandise, invitations to special events, and recognition in each book and on our website.

In addition to donations, we rely on subscriptions from readers like you to provide an invaluable ongoing investment in Deep Vellum that demonstrates a commitment to our editorial vision and mission. Subscribers are the bedrock of our support as we grow the readership for these amazing works of literature from every corner of the world. The investment our subscribers make allows us to demonstrate to potential donors and bookstores alike the support and demand for Deep Vellum's literature across a broad readership and gives us the ability to grow our mission in ever-new, ever-innovative ways.

In partnership with our sister company and bookstore, Deep Vellum Books, located in the historic cultural district of Deep Ellum in central Dallas, we organize and host literary programming such as author readings, translator workshops, creative writing classes, spoken word performances, and interdisciplinary arts events for writers, translators, and artists from across the globe. Our goal is to enrich and connect the world through the power of the written and spoken word, and we have been recognized for our efforts by being named one of the "Five Small Presses Changing the Face of the Industry" by *Flavorwire* and honored as Dallas's Best Publisher by *D Magazine*.

If you would like to get involved with Deep Vellum as a donor, subscriber, or volunteer, please contact us at deepvellum.org. We would love to hear from you.

Thank you all. Enjoy reading.
Will Evans Founder & Publisher Deep Vellum Publishing

LIGA DE ORO ($5,000+)

Anonymous (2)

LIGA DEL SIGLO ($1,000+)

Allred Capital Management
Ben & Sharon Fountain
Judy Pollock
Life in Deep Ellum
Loretta Siciliano
Lori Feathers
Mary Ann Thompson-Frenk
   & Joshua Frenk
Matthew Rittmayer
Meriwether Evans
Pixel and Texel
Nick Storch
Social Venture Partners Dallas
Stephen Bullock

DONORS

Adam Rekerdres
Alan Shockley
Amrit Dhir
Anonymous
Andrew Yorke
Anthony Messenger
Bob Appel
Bob & Katherine Penn
Brandon Childress
Brandon Kennedy
Caroline Casey
Charles Dee Mitchell
Charley Mitcherson
Cheryl Thompson
Christie Tull
Daniel J. Hale

Ed Nawotka
Rev. Elizabeth
   & Neil Moseley
Ester & Matt Harrison
Grace Kenney
Greg McConeghy
Jeff Waxman
JJ Italiano
Justin Childress
Kay Cattarulla
Kelly Falconer
Linda Nell Evans
Lissa Dunlay
Marian Schwartz
   & Reid Minot
Mark Haber

Mary Cline
Maynard Thomson
Michael Reklis
Mike Kaminsky
Mokhtar Ramadan
Nikki & Dennis Gibson
Olga Kislova
Patrick Kukucka
Richard Meyer
Steve Bullock
Suejean Kim
Susan Carp
Susan Ernst
Theater Jones
Tim Perttula
Tony Thomson

SUBSCRIBERS

Alan Shockley
Aldo Sanchez
Anita Tarar
Audrey Mash
Ben Fountain
Ben Nichols
Bradford Pearson
Charles Dee Mitchell
Chase Marcella
Chris Sweet
Christie Tull
Courtney Sheedy
David Christensen
David Travis
David Weinberger
Dori Boone-Costantino
Elaine Corwin
Farley Houston
Ghassan Fergiani
Guilty Dave Bristow
Horatiu Matei

James Tierney
Janine Allen
Jeanne Milazzo
Jeffrey Collins
Jessa Crispin
Joe Milazzo
John O'Neill
John Schmerein
John Winkelman
Joshua Edwin
Julie Janicke Muhsmann
Karen Olsson
Kasie Henderson
Kimberly Alexander
Kristopher Phillips
Marcia Lynx Qualey
Margaret Terwey
Martha Gifford
Meaghan Corwin
Michael Elliott
Michael Filippone

Michael Norton
Michael Wilson
Mies de Vries
Mike Kaminsky
Neal Chuang
Nick Oxford
Nicola Molinaro
Peter McCambridge
Ryan Jones
Shelby Vincent
Stephanie Barr
Steven Kornajcik
Steven Norton
Susan Ernst
Tim Kindseth
Tim Looney
Todd Jailer
Tony Messenger
Whitney Leader-Picone
Will Pepple
William Jarrell

COMING FALL/SPRING 2016–2017 FROM DEEP VELLUM

CARMEN BOULLOSA · *Heavens on Earth*
translated by Shelby Vincent · MEXICO

ANANDA DEVI · *Eve Out of Her Ruins*
translated by Jeffrey Zuckerman · MAURITIUS

JÓN GNARR · *The Outlaw*
translated by Lytton Smith· ICELAND

CLAUDIA SALAZAR JIMÉNEZ · *Blood of the Dawn*
translated by Elizabeth Bryer · PERU

JOSEFINE KLOUGART · *Of Darkness*
translated by Martin Aitken · DENMARK

SERGIO PITOL · *The Magician of Vienna*
translated by George Henson · MEXICO

EDUARDO RABASA · *A Zero-Sum Game*
translated by Christina MacSweeney · MEXICO

BAE SUAH · *Recitation*
translated by Deborah Smith · SOUTH KOREA

JUAN RULFO · *The Golden Cockerel & Other Writings*
translated by Douglas J. Weatherford · MEXICO

ANNE GARRÉTA · *Not One Day*
translated by Emma Ramadan · FRANCE

YANICK LAHENS · *Moonbath*
translated by Emily Gogolak · HAITI

DEEP
VELLUM